T0319238

The Mother of My Child

Wilfred Ndum Akombi

Langaa Research & Publishing CIG
Mankon, Bamenda

Publisher:
Langaa RPCIG
Langaa Research & Publishing Common Initiative Group
P.O. Box 902 Mankon
Bamenda
North West Region
Cameroon
Langaagrp@gmail.com
www.langaa-rpcig.net

Distributed in and outside N. America by African Books Collective
orders@africanbookscollective.com
www.africanbookcollective.com

ISBN:9956-579-82-3

© Wilfred Ndum Akombi 2011

DISCLAIMER
All views expressed in this publication are those of the author and do not
necessarily reflect the views of Langaa RPCIG.

Chapter One

That night, we stood at the balcony of Blue Ladies. From there, one could gaze the various activities along the riverside. It was dark but from light reflection, we could see it all clearly. Every young German, even those at the age of twelve, was always eager to go dancing on weekends with a love one. Smoking and spitting on the streets, lip-singing music that they listened through their headsets and dancing as they walk was the major behaviour. They could wear t-shirts, jeans trousers pulled halfway down, and their caps facing back. To deny any teenager from this activity was like denying him the right to breathe.

'Baco,' Stoney tapped me on the shoulders pointing down the River Rhein arena. Just near the river, a tall lady after a kiss, bent and a man hurriedly pulled down his trousers. As she bent holding the ground like rolling forward, the object between her thighs protruded backwards. He held the lady's hips and with the enigma of a man with high erotic hunger began to do it.

'Hey, oh, it's so good,' wailed the lady in a tiny voice. It was total shit.

No one could dispute the fact that such an enjoyment completely dislodged her bones. We suddenly heard a high romantic wailing from another corner. As if that was what was going to safe the world from sin, just like never before, the people were as busy as soldier ants.

'Listen, they're killing another bitch that way. She's crying,' I said. Though things chilled my bones, I was going wet and hungry too. The whole environment was lurked with chaotic romance.

Blue Ladies was a nightclub that ranked amongst the best of clubs in the whole of Northwest. It was at the second floor of that storey building with well-furnished balconies and tinted banisters. The attractive structure stood near the river Rhein that cut across the neighbourhood. One would step

1

out to the playground down stairs to relax with a lady, either spilling kisses or exercising the waist. Some others too were soothing the verdant chests of some ladies.

'Baco, she was the one wailing,' said Stoney pointing at a lady downstairs. Her steps could better explain and testify she was the one lovely screaming or could be one of them.

'Of course,' I confirmed looking at her passing by into the club. I gulped a mouthful of spit.

'I should have been the one,' I thought aloud not knowing that it got to Stoney's ears.

'What? You mean rock the bitch?'

'Oh, yes, I feel like doing so too,' I said. There was no miracle that night but just like *if you call the devil, he will be around,* the instigations were high.

A Lady suddenly came out of the hall for a cigarette break. My eyes dived into hers. She dragged from a cigarette, held it and in smoke bubbles sent it out into the air. Then, she looked at me again. She was not just fat but she was extra large, and appeared desperate.

'Approach that vast one. She is looking at you.' Stoney said. He was a timid boy but would always encourage. He smashed my shoes as he whispered to me.

'Yes, my boy, I will take action,' I responded.

My heart was pumping several times per millisecond. I moved forward to the lady.

'Hi. Fine baby, how are you doing?'

'Well, I don't know,' she doubted.

'Can we get in for a sound or two?'

'Well, well…' She shrugged.

I swayed my head from side to side waiting for her to drop the cigarette. Stoney watched us from the other end of the balcony.

In the ball, I held her waist and then we rolled round a small corner. My hands got her blinded and she was feeling the touch right into her head. For sure, she must have been staved for a long time. The music was at the climax. No touch could irritate her. From her upper side, my right fingers moved down to her backside. Wow! Quite a beautiful moment! The lights were dim. The hall was in total romance.

'Oh my God,' I thought. Her whole head fell backwards as if she was giving everything to me in great enjoyment. She appeared to be too high and it was like she had taken some considerable amount of alcohol. The hot sound was over but the hall was humming, like a computer booting, waiting for another sound to follow. She took a seat just nearby.

'Thanks,' I said as I waved to her.

I walked towards the other side to meet Stoney.

'My man,' he said, 'I saw how you were digging it out.'

'That lady yearns to have me but she's too fat.'

'Too fat? Except you do not know what you're looking for. Those very fat ones can easily give you protection in this country. They can easily give in for marriage.'

'You're right, Stoney, but...'

'What? Don't fuck up with that bitch. You've got it.'

'Yes my guy, we'll see about that.'

Stoney couldn't let it drop.

'I mean you get her telephone number. Have you done so?'

'No.'

'Get it now. Maybe she is shy to give or to ask yours.'

I walked to her in panic.

'Hi, fine lady, how can I contact you some other time?'

'You mean my number?'

'Yes, if you don't mind!'

Then a flashy smile came from her lips though her red face maintained a solemn mode. Perhaps, the fug that lurked the whole place made her uncomfortable. She hurriedly gave the number as one seizing an opportunity else it died off. I walked out to meet Stoney who stood at the balcony.

'Have you gotten her contact number?'

'Oh, yes.'

I looked at the number several times. It was like a big

booty.

'You see, everything is achievable. This means you'll be the first amongst us to taste a white lady. Did you kiss her?'

'No, the population… I only caressed.'

'Caressed what?'

I wanted to explain but a man smoking just besides us stared at me. I was equally shy then like Stoney.

'We will talk about that when home,' I said as I raised my head to see if she still sat at the corner. Her head was screwing from side to side across the hall.

'I think she is looking for us.'

'Sure,' Stoney shrugged in doubts.

'Really,' I confirmed looking at her in the fumbling.

We still decided to remain outside for the reason that the air in wasn't fresh enough. The number of people stepping out down towards the play arena began to increase.

'Baco, register the number in your mobile phone or you risk misplacing it.'

As I bent to register the number, I saw her descending the stairs. She held the banister and turned to look if I was still watching her. We held eyes for several seconds and she smiled. I descended towards her.

'Hello Tina, are you retiring home?'

'Yes, please. When do I call you?'

'Tomorrow,' I responded with a smile.

'What time precisely?'

'Ehmm, ehm… At ten.'

'I'll be delighted. I will call,' she said waving goodbye. I saw her walking towards a red Mercedes car and it soon revived its engine for few minutes. Then it gradually disappeared into the streets. I immediately ascended to meet Stoney. He cheered up jokingly and was so excited about the whole show like never in a lifetime. Perhaps, he thought if it could happen to me, then it was possible for him too.

'You know, she has driven off in a Mercedes car.'

'So she came by car! That's great!' exclaimed Stoney

astonished. 'Then she must be a big girl. She is a fruitful lady with who you can make good time. You're damn fortunate.'

Blue Ladies was aging out for that night. A few young boys came holding hands with their loved ones and bottles of beer and cigarettes. Some were like drunk. They could take their girls by the arm, holding a beer in the right and dragging from a cigarette with the left. Indeed, it was their life and they were making great use of it. A young boy of fifteen walked aggressively from the hall with a bottle of whisky also holding a cigarette. He drank a great quantity and spat it on couples that were kissing. One of them hit him on the face. He fell to the ground. 'Du bist eine ashloch,' he said still struggling to get up. 'Was bist du? Alkoholiker,' the boy fired back ready to hit him again. It didn't take long when the security boys took him away.

The sides of the river were attractive. They were nice looking with carved painted stones. There were painted wooden seats placed there for people to sit during leisure time. It was a good site for lovers to sit in the day and discuss love. It was what young idle Germans do. During the day one could see small boats transporting coal and other related goods. In addition, there were many tourists on board ships, enjoying life. Amongst other cities, the river also cut across Düsseldorf, a business town in the Northwest of Germany. The area near *Blue Ladies* nightclub was special. It was just at the heart of the city.

Preposterous ladies on call used to come around, sometimes about the hours of six and seven, searching for customers to do blow jobs. Old people who couldn't do it the normal way used to pay them highly to keep them warm, sometimes the whole night. Police used to storm such areas to trap ladies who were prostituting without licence, since prostitution had become a legal business.

The reason most prostitutes were lingering the riverside more this time than before was the fact that the place zoned for them was getting congested. It was a free zone near a zoo, just a kilometre away from the riverside.

The zoo prostitution arena was a two-acre land with wild flowers. People would come and bid prices and would do it in cars or often chauffeured to a customer's house. Sometimes, they used to render the services at the same place in their cars.

As we descended to leave, we heard snapping sounds from kissing lips. Many could be seen bent and doing it the way dogs would do. Others were digging it out in their cars. That was the gospel truth.

We left the club and made our way through the terraces. The only thought in me was that the night was quite symbolic. It would be a memorable night.

'We have to be here again next week,' said Stoney. 'Maybe some fortune will fall too on my way.'

* * *

That night, I dreamed three times. All the dreams were wet. It was dawn when I turned my lucky self. My heart was beating abnormally. I woke up and stood beside the window, watching people on the street already going on with their daily activities. At the sight of any stocky lady, my heart would pump double and my mind would only take me back to that moment at the club. Stoney was still in bed. I walked closer to the mirror and stood watching my lips. I was just thinking how I would kiss Tina. How would a white woman taste? The question would have its answer sooner, as I thought. Stoney woke from sleep.

'It'll soon be ten. I'm expecting that call. I doubt whether she is going to ring as promised.'

'Why not… I tell you most of their boys don't like them because they are too fat. Be not surprised, she hasn't tasted a man for last two years. Believe me.' My heart was beating until it started arching as time was drawing near. Stoney would not let me think of the achievement, as he said,

6

'Sometimes, fat girls are good in bed. They are soft and warm. But the too tiny ones are hard.' He laughed.

'For me, I can do that but not to get coupled up for life.'

'What if she proposes marriage?'

'Stoney, you know the answer to that question. If it happens, it is just a flirting business of a thing. How can that be for life when Nicoline is there? She will never be disappointed. Not in this life. She is so indispensable in my life.'

Nicoline was my girlfriend back home. I had decided to get her hand in marriage. I loved her and saw nothing on earth that could encumber our relationship.

'If Nicoline hears that you've already started fishing a white girl, she can commit suicide.'

My mobile phone vibrated and I hurriedly picked.

'Is that Baco?'

'Yes,' I replied.

'How are you doing? I am Tina, the girl you met yesterday at *Blue Ladies*.'

'I'm very fine, thank you. How are you doing too?'

We discussed for several minutes and then she said to me, 'I am happy I met you yesterday.' In a typical gay and hungry voice, she made a rendezvous and I would meet her at Kama street number 10 at 8 pm.

Chapter Two

J ust like others, that evening was full of activity as the streets were jamb to capacity. I traced Tina's door. While at the main door, I placed my finger on the bell to ring but my heart was beating so much that within seconds, my armpits sweated. In that fumbling suffocation, I changed the hand and touched the bell with the left but still, was unable to ring. I relaxed and walked around for some five minutes.

There was an old woman watching my actions through a window. I saw her as I raised my heard up the high buildings just opposite. If I failed in my second attempt to ring, she could call the police. That was the habit of most old men and women. Most of such people had no children with them. Their children at maturity had the right to live anywhere and anyhow they wanted. They lived alone in greatest idleness and boredom. Sometimes, they would hate to see young girls and boys holding hands. As if regretting that they were old, they would also curse the young ones. Thus, one of their wilful jobs was to help call the police at the sight of any obscure activity on the streets, especially when it concerned a foreigner.

When I saw the old woman staring at me, I immediately pressed the bell again. There was a successive buzz up stairs.

'Who is there?' she asked.

'Please, open. It's Baco.'

She freed the door from up. I pushed it open and ascended with fright. At the second floor, I traced the door written on it *Tina*. It was half way open. Still, I rang. 'Please, it's open. Come in,' she said adjusting her weighty buttocks on a chair behind an upright piano.

'Hi.'

'Hi,' she said ushering me to a seat. Her eyes for several seconds never reached mine. She managed to smile though with her eyes focused on the key board. I was still shy and to return the smile was a little hard. It could take time to familiarise myself with the strange environment.

'I am singing a song for my dog,' she said.

'A song for your dog!'

I spoke no word again when she answered in the affirmative. How would someone spend time singing for a dog? Wasn't that crazy?

'Markus, come here,' she said to the dog. A huge black dog heaved itself from under the table and waxed its tail rushing into her legs. I hated dogs and cats but the first impression I had of her was that she was fond of petting dogs as a pastime. The beefy dog almost put its snout into her legs like looking for something to lick.

'Markus, nein. Sitzen,' she said and the dog crouched down under the piano with fallen ears like one deprived of something that had been a routine.

'Baco, can you try a piano?' she asked.

'No. I can try a guitar.' It was then that I managed a little smile.

A few minutes later, she closed the piano looking relieved.

'You would love some chocolate, I hope.'

'No problem,' I shrugged.

She saw a little doubt on my face. I would have loved something heavier but for the fact that I was not familiar to her.

'Maybe some fruit juice...'

'Any of them is still alright.'

She took out a carton of juice with two glasses. As she bent down to place them on the table, her blouse relaxed from her breasts and part of it exposed. She sat on the same sofa on my right and filled the glasses though all half, then sipped twice and looked at me.

'So how is life treating you?'

'God is great.'

'How old are you, if you don't mind?

'I'm twenty five.'

10

She was quiet for some five minutes. I almost regretted for I thought I should have added some more five years to meet up with her age. I estimated hers to be thirty or more.

'I am twenty,' she said. I turned and looked at her freckled face. It was shocking. There was no sign of lies on it. She appeared candid but her age never matched with the huge body beside me. She raised her glass to give me a drink. I sipped it once. Her own was more sweet and soft though all from the same carton. After several minutes together, she looked at me with great romance.

'You're a handsome guy. Can I kiss you?' I could feel a panic in her.

'Thanks for the compliment. You're also beautiful. Feel free to kiss me.'

She held my head from behind and our lips glued. After a couple of minutes, she moved her right hand towards the buckle and her dress dropped on the floor. She was like fumbling in suffocation. Indeed, she was on heat. The dog barked as we rolled on the carpet. That kind of thing had never happened in my life. How could a man go to bed with a woman on the very first day? This time, even the thought that there was a killer disease never came to me, nor the thought that one could use a contraceptive. What a damn shame!

She hissed at Markus, as it barked again. As she turned to stop Markus, I saw her red string. My body was in anxiety. She took my hand and we walked natural into the room. We were there in bed.

'Eh... the dog has climbed,' I said shaking her. She slapped it and picked up a silver ruler from the side cupboard to scare it. It carved out into the sitting room. She took back the same position. It was nasty what we were doing, but we kept on. My body was in confusion. At some short moment, I was like one at a comma. It was a strange ecstasy. If at this time God was as wicked as men are, He would simply pour acid on us. However, as I thought, He stood watching, waiting and ready to forgive that grave trespass.

11

After five minutes, I was exhausted. She walked into the parlour and brought out an erotica. She appeared to be a lady of serious and extravagant erotic appetite. There were many styles in the erotica. The one that sent a chill down my spine was a dog licking in between a lady's legs. She pointed at it and asked, 'Have you seen this before?'

'What?' I asked in astonishment. Indeed, it was a bombshell.

'Don't be scared,' she said. 'It's just for fun.'

She was guilty. As she opened other pictures, her right leg crossed on mine. She was hot and we did it again. For sure, what I poured in her must have driven her into extreme hallucinations. Nothing could convince me that she had not been in such a starvation for several years.

It was 11 pm, as I sat on the sofa. She was still in the room searching her car keys.

'How could I have to adore a lady on the first occasion?' I thought still.

'Can't you make the night here?' she asked.

'No, some other time. I must go.'

'I hope you come tomorrow. I have much affection for you.'

'I will do.'

We descended the building. In her car, we drove off. As she drove slowly, she took out a CD and slotted it in. The voice of Celine Dion sang a soft sweet love song. She too lip sang it. It was *Declaration of Love*.

She was almost approaching the camp as she slowed and stopped. Some people were still roaming the streets. The car idled just a hundred and fifty metres from the camp. The sound was still on.

'Do you love music madly?' she asked

'I do but not always.'

'Celine Dion is my favourite singer. I like her love songs. Which kind of music do you enjoy most?'

'I love freedom Reggae songs.'

'Why so?' she asked surprised.

'I do because there is no self-determination on the planet earth. There is no fairness. Humankind is in continuous pains and through singing reggae, they help fight the abuse.'

Just as if she was not interested in what I was saying, she continued singing the song.

'I must go,' I said almost opening the door.

'Wait for some two minutes. Let's enjoy this sound together. Why are you in haste?' she said and switched off the light, then kissed my lips several times. A few seconds after, she switched on the light and looked at my face. Though Tina was fat, she had a nice face. She switched it off again and lured my head backwards while kissing me. I was slack for I was not in the mood. The more, I was exhausted. I slid out of the car.

'Baco, we see tomorrow,' she said relaxed like one who has won a contract.

'Good night too,' I waved. She drove off. I walked sluggishly to the camp. Stoney waited and was already asleep. When I entered, he woke up.

'My God, what time is it?' he asked.

'It's twelve and above.'

Stoney was a very funny person.

'Baco, you're stinking of that thing. You must take a bath this night otherwise you poison the environment.' I smiled. Though he was just joking, there was some truth in it. 'How many rounds did you make?' he continued.

'I did nothing,' I said smiling but my face expressed it all.

'When are you to meet her again?'

'She says tomorrow. Maybe, I will make the night there.'

'That's just what I want to hear. Make hay at the bright sun. You need to hurry and get her store soaked as fast as possible. We don't know what the government is preparing to do with us. By then, she might have bore a branch that you can hang on. I mean you get her pregnant without any waste of time.'

'Really, the influx of strangers this time can easily irritate those holding the yams and the knives.'

I left for the bathroom for a shower. We spent the whole night discussing the triumph. In an hour or so, it was soon to get dawn. It didn't mean much. At least, something was in the making.

'If Nicoline hears this, she isn't going to be comfortable.'

'She should if it happens. If I have a German stay, it will be for our own good.'

'You mean bring her here?'

'Straight away,' I said. 'I just have to fuck Tina's asshole off with her baby and settle down with my heart. That's all.'

Stoney was my intimate friend since back home. The court had turned down his application for a residence permit but his lawyer had made an appeal at a higher court. He was at the greatest dilemma, whether to accept the proposal of Margeret to pay the sum of ten thousand Euros for a contract marriage or to sign that he was the father of the soon to born baby by Mittags. Mittags was a German in love with one Sunday, a Nigerian. They had had a first child and because of that, a German stay was issued to Sunday. The second child was then a good business. She had proposed the sum of five thousand Euros for Stoney to pay but he was still contemplating.

If he had to accept the contract with Margeret, it meant they had to reside together.

It was dawn. We spent the whole time discussing about paternity rights. Stoney decided to meet Margeret later that day to plead if she could accept a lesser amount. It was coincidental that she resided at same street with Tina.

'Tina shouldn't know about this,' Stoney said.

'I can understand you. I know they are freakish like their weather.'

'She might be aware of the sham and hypocrisy in their society, yet, she knows you're out for true love.'

Later, we took off for Margeret's. She was a fifty five year old woman. She had divorced at the age of thirty and mothered a girl by name Lucy, a very beautiful lady.

On the way, while relaxed walking to Margeret's, I prayed that we never met Lucy with her mother. 'Who are the boys so courageous to stand before Lucy to ask for her hand in love?' asked Stoney.

'Are there no courageous boys out there? It needs not money, nor handsomeness to win a beautiful hand. It takes simple courage.'

'If I can have just a single opportunity to touch that bloomy cheek, that chubby jaw, I have to raise my head to the heavens.'

'Not at all Stoney... It's useless building on sand. That's a fruitless dream, not that it's impossible, but because it would be difficult to have the occasion to talk to her. More to that, I don't think we are here for beauty or out for love. We are out to better our lives through their women.'

We were soon at Margeret's door. Stoney pressed the bell once and she said, 'Ja bitte.'

'It's me, Stoney.'

We pushed as it buzzed. We met her in with a cat as huge as a tiger. She was soothing its back and kissing it. From a window behind us, one could see the high structures right to the train station. The construction of Kama Street was perfect. She could see anyone approaching the building from far through her window.

I raised my head to pictures on the wall. There, were the pictures of a man, those of Margeret, a dog and a cat. There were also pictures of some other people, I guessed, were family members. She served us with some fruit juice from the fridge. As we were sipping from the glasses, she was preparing food for her dog and cat.

'Please, just give me some time. I have to prepare some food for Miki and Titi,' she said.

'Take your time,' said Stoney.'

When she finished, she introduced her collection.

Margeret was beautiful though old age was fast in consuming her beauty. Still, I know she must have gladdened many hearts in her days when she was young. When she finished introducing the pictures, she said, 'So how is the country treating you people?'

'There is no need to ask such a question,' said Stoney, 'for everyone is aware. We're breathing fire.'

'Really, I know what people like you should be passing through,' she confirmed. 'Even the law makers are trapped. That is the biggest irony in the whole show.' She paused and looked at Stoney.

'I hope you have accepted the ten thousand Euros?' she asked.

'I thought you could make some considerations. You know I'm in the refugee camp and have no right to work.' Stoney pleaded. She wasn't happy with that.

'Let me tell you something, young man. I just want to accept this sum because of the good friend who connected you to me. We've done this business with her for several years and she knows the usual amount. If it was in the years back, I could accept something lesser than that. Now things are tough and people search for these opportunities madly. If you're not capable, I can look for another customer. The last contract was for thirteen thousand. You can imagine.'

At length, no one spoke, as they were all trying to think about the whole business. 'This is even the last time I am doing this business. At least, I've made some money from the risky thing…There are other young people out there using work permits of others to earn a living. You have to do what you can to make money. Look for some one and arrange to use his papers and you'll find life so easy.'

She waited for Stoney to say a word but he was still.

'If you're not cheered up, tell me.' She said frowning and at the same time, exhaled smoke through her nose.

'Not that,' Stoney responded. 'I'll see what to do next week to start the papers.'

'Know that,' she added, 'you have to spend most of your time here. You also have to bring most of your dresses here or you mar the whole thing when it reaches the Police. They are fond of surprising couples to see if the celebrated marriage was done in good faith.'

My telephone rang and I whipped it up. It was Tina. I never wanted to talk to her for the fact that Margeret was present.

'Please I will call you in next thirty minutes,' I said and clicked off the phone. Somebody rang Margeret's bell. She opened the door as if she knew who was there. It was Lucy.

'Hi,' she greeted us. We answered in chorus. My heart trembled. My fear was what to do if we caught eyes. Hence, I was careful the way I looked. She sat near the dinning table and spoke with her mother in German. I could here but not understand. What they discussed remained to them but I guessed she made a statement concerning the business because she pointed at us. Lucy walked out. I aimed to catch sight of her hips, but she was gone.

Margeret broke the deep silence of serious admiration.

'So we have concluded,' she said yawning.

'Yes I hope. I have to involve a lawyer,' said Stoney. 'The foreign office has been looking for documents to send me back home. If I hand a passport carelessly, they can use it to deport me immediately.'

'You don't get dreaded. I am a German. It can only be too difficult if it's a foreigner getting married to you. You only have to advance some money and I will take care of the rest.'

'Then, I think the whole business has started,' Stoney concluded.

That evening, we knew we had a step forward. Stoney would soon deposit documents for his marriage deal and I had just had Tina. Still, that was not the heart of the issue. Depositing documents for processing a marriage was the biggest risk one could think of.

As we approached the camp, I saw the door open.

'Didn't we close the door?' Stoney asked.

'I did key it.'

'Who must have opened it then?'

'Maybe the caretaker,' I said walking faster to see who was there. We met a boy of enormous muscles waiting.

'Hi,' he said. 'I was brought here by the caretaker of the camp.' He was a fresh asylum seeker just received into the camp.

'You are welcomed,' I said though not happy. The Two metres square room was too small for even a single person. But at this time it was to house three, and maybe another would add.

'From where do you come?' Stoney asked.

'I'm a Nigerian,' he said.

'What's your name?'

'I'm 'Chinedu Peter.'

'I'm Stoney and this is my room mate Baco. We all come from Cameroon. It's so regrettable they've transferred you here,' said Stoney. 'To be transferred to this camp as a permanent place to stay while your application is being studied is total condemnation to hell. It's not easy.'

'Well, one is already in the mess,' he said.

'That's the reason you see the camp too full.'

'Stoney,' I said, 'you don't need to frighten people because individuals have their luck. Situations do vary from person to person.'

'I didn't mean to scare him. He's already in the mess and I must tell him the fact. The only way out, Mr. Chinedu, is to enter a lady's legs. That is the only place that the lawmakers have kept opened. It's the simplest means of having a stay in this country. If you're a good man who can sex well, then be sure one fucking bitch will keep you protected. Either get engaged in marriage or impregnate her so as to have the papers. That's just the messy game.'

Chinedu was too hard on the face. The only thing that

made him looked nice was his head combed backwards. Though he said he just entered the country, it was hard to believe.

'I don't believe you,' said Stoney, 'because you mix a lot of German words in your discussion.'

'I learned German in Nigeria before travelling.'

'Tell us you've been hanging around in the acrobatic way. There are many people like that in the city hiding from the police. Some have been living illegally for five years or more.'

The issue of the room being too small never bordered me. I knew I could make most of the nights at Tina's apartment. Chinedu would be master of the house, I thought. The building was like a dormitory. There was a long tiny passageway and each room faced the other, about fifty rooms altogether. Some contained about five persons and some others were more. It was a good example of a cosmopolitan society. There were both laymen and intellectuals from many nations. There were Muslims, Christians and those of other faiths or denominations. There were illiterates, bookmen, school dropouts, as well as civilised and uncivilised people.

The caretaker would come from time to time to see whether things were in order, or to take note of those who were irregular in the camp. This was the kind of report forwarded to the foreign office daily. Nobody was to move out of the city except on permission. Some had been there for seven and some others about eight years. They had all never moved out of this location due to the lone fact that they never had a residence permit. In case of an abuse of all these rigid rules, was a penalty that ranged from suspension of ones temporary identification card, no food money for that month, and other petite punishments.

If only the world knew the experiences of the people, it would surely fast, pray for the Heavens to create and sacrifice another son, as was the case of Jesus. *Germany is just empty name* some had described. *It has a powerful economy, but the individuals are in serious starvation.*

Taxes were increasing gravely but incomes were falling. That was the simple reason many Germans were investing in other countries around Europe. Many Afro-Germans were migrating to the UK while others were leaving for the US. For the past years, like clouds on mountain tops in times of no winds, we would wonder the streets and the train stations. Only a few fortunate ones, like one out of a hundred had the right to work. Some people in the camp, who came young, were going grey. They came there at their forties. Still, they waited patiently for the courts to take their decisions. Yet, their patience was like that of a dog waiting for bones under a vegetable stand.

It was time we were preparing for bed after our evening meal. My mobile phone rang. It was Tina.

'Yes, *Schatz*. How are you doing?' Tina asked.

'I'm fine, and you?'

'Baby, I'm so worried,' said Tina. 'You said you were to call back but I've not heard from you. Are you alright?'

'Tina, I'm fine but I can only see you tomorrow.'

'Okay sweetie. You should know that I love you so much that I can't do without.'

She kissed me on the phone and then the voice was off. In bed, we spent the first hour talking about Lucy's beauty. Her beauty made me measure what Tina was. I only consoled myself that I was out for an intention. Otherwise, she was supposed to pay me a disgrace fee allowance. It was hard to say but she was really out of structure. In the real sense of things, she was out of human shape.

Chapter Three

It had become a tradition of thinking and discussing mostly about residence permits.

Another month came. The sun rushed and was soon disappearing behind the tall structures. I decided to go to Tina through a short course. From the camp through the streets, I went towards the train station. From there to Tina was just a short distance. The station was one of the most guarded places in the country. Police officers lingered there daily because people were also using it for other purposes. It was a meeting point for those selling cocaine and other related none accepted issues. Due to the rise in world terrorism, security had suddenly doubled.

If one lingered around the train station for several minutes, the police would control him. It was a large station with twelve rails, which they called *Gleise*. Beneath the rails were buried rooms meant for station shops, toilets, small restaurants, ticket offices and information centres. The Police would sit in their office with surveillance cameras watching the movements of people. Other officers kept walking up and down the station for top security.

While at the station, I caught sight with a friend I had known some times back. He was wondering on rail five. He waved to me and I walked towards him. The station was busy. People were thudding the steps from under where it was like a tunnel up to the rails where one could be able to enter a train. As well, others were dropping from the trains and descending the stairs.

'What's up boy?' he greeted. 'It's been a long time since we met.'

'Really, it's been a long time. I am very fine. How are you doing?'

'I thank God,' he said. 'I just want to rush to the next stop. I have a rendezvous with a job agency today. I just want to respect it and see if things can be fruitful.'

'Did you apply for the job with your papers?' This, I said in whisper because it was an illegal affair.

'Yes, I just want to keep trying. This is the second year I've been trying but it's not that easy. Sometimes, the agency offers the job but the authorities in our location don't permit me do it.'

'Why spend time on impossibilities? The only thing you can do is to use some one's permanent work permit to look for a job. You can then give him a small percentage of the earnings. Do you think they want us to work any longer? An asylum seeker in this land is a dead human being.'

'I know bros,' said the friend. 'They want us to live on the small amount and at same place. Even a dog needs to walk around freely. It needs freedom.'

'Time has been so cruel to people. Rather than driving us into a 21st century of hope, it is driving us backwards to the darkest days of the 1940s, when even Jewish corpses were beaten by the German *Führer* forces.'

As we talked, there was an interruption from behind. A tall man in a coffee brown jacket and chocolate brown khaki tapped me on the shoulders. It was a policeman. Another was approaching from the other end as if they wanted to make sure none of us could escape.

'Hallo,' he said, 'Passport, please.' It was a serious awkwardness. I hated the sudden change of scene. I equally hated the police officers with all my heart. It was unfortunate that I had forgotten my temporary resident permit at home. The friend handed an old torn green paper to the officer. It seemed to have been renewed for hundred of times. The officer whipped out a telephone from his pockets and made some calls as he looked on the paper. He soon handed it to him and stretched his hand to me.

'Sir, I'm Baco. Sorry I've forgotten my identification papers at home.' He immediately dropped his phone in his pockets and took out a pair of handcuffs. The other officer immediately gripped me from the trouser band. In handcuffs, they tugged me passed the rushing crowd and then into a small room, some one hundred metres away from the main rails. At the downer exit of the station was a little slope. A small building like a secret place for the police delved into the slope. They opened the door and forced me in. It was really dark inside but the lights automatically switched on. The stillness inside could deceive one that there was no live outside. I guess the walls were about a metre thick and rocky. I saw other doors leading downwards like some rooms were underground. For sure, there were secret dungeons underground.

Even a blast could not destroy the complicated buried structure.

On the walls were handcuffs, whips, teargas bottles, flashlights and other equipments that the quaking situation did not permit me study. They commanded me to undress. I almost hesitated but I realised there was some danger. I took off my jean trousers and T-shirt. One of them wore his gloves. Like one opening the segments of an orange, he held my buttocks and opened my anus. He sent his index finger right inside. Then after, he asked me to open my mouth and with same index finger, turned my tongue up and down to make sure there was nothing inside.

'What is your name?' he asked. After they wrote it down and took my fingerprints on a piece of paper. They saw nothing wrong.

'You can go,' he said after several calls made. I hated myself at that moment to have allowed them finger my anus.

I couldn't go through the station for many people had seen me dragged as an ardent criminal. I took a different course going round to reach Tina. On the way, what crowded my mind was a picture of policemen fingering anuses. I rang and Tina opened. I never waited for her to say 'Sit down.' There was a big glow of anger wailing in me.

'Are you alright?' she asked.

'I am.' She was not satisfied with the response.

'Why do you wear this kind of sour face and tell me all is well?' I was completely silent.

'Lady, you don't have to be troubled. I'm not happy because the police have just molested me at the train station. They took me to their private place, searched me and fingered my anus brutally.'

'Why did they do that?' she asked. 'Maybe they thought you are illegal.'

'So they control illegal people by putting fingers into their anuses!'

'Well,' she fumbled in a little smile, 'maybe they thought of cocaine. You have to forget of them and think only of your life otherwise, you poison your mind.'

However, I was gradually becoming familiar with her.

'I suppose you make the night here,' she said.

'Why?' I pretended. For this, she was a little upset.

'Darling, don't ask this kind of a question. You know I love you so much.' I remained silent but knew she wanted at least a word. After a couple of seconds, I couldn't pretend anymore. I looked at her and she caught me in a smile.

'Don't worry I'll be here tonight,' I said. She fumbled in greatest happiness walking towards me and with her right knee, pushed my legs as I leaned on the sofa. I held her hips and she too held my head lulling it backwards and forward. I moved my hands up and down her hills and right up her spinal code, then down again right to her laps.

'Baco,' she confessed, 'you're so indispensable in my life now. It's hard to hide my feelings. You might not understand what I mean.' I could feel how a desperate lady was getting frustrated.

I was still out to confirm her words. I raised my head and looked at her queerly.

'Say you know me and not that you love me.'

'Baco,' she emphasised, 'I really do love you. Don't ruin my dreams. Don't say words that can dry off one's love sap.' Her eyes were wet. She raised my head with her hands so that my eyes fixed on hers.

'Baby,' she cried, 'if there is something you want me to do so that you can believe that I love you, please, just tell me and consider it done. I remained quiet though my hands still gripped her waist. She had relaxed her hands just because she wanted to make things serious.

'For how many days today you know me that you want to take oath?'

'It doesn't matter that we just knew each other,' she said like pleading. 'Maybe you're just scorning at me and not that you doubt my love for you. Just tell me what to do to show I love you whole heartedly. I have been dreaming to have a guy like you for a few years now.'

'Buy me a plane if you want,' I said. She smiled and responded, 'Even Darby and Joan never arrived at that level.'

Tina's flat was well furnished. Her dresses were expensive though none ever fitted her squarely. There was a TV set in the sitting room, another in her bedroom and one too in Markus's tiny place. In the sitting room was also an upright piano near a cupboard full with luxurious utensils- gold wine flutes, diamond beer tumblers, kettles of various kinds and others.

'This lady must have been living in affluence,' I thought. I almost asked her but I took my time.

'Baby, do you like some chocolate?' she asked and I answered in the affirmative. She dashed into the kitchen as if I was running. Then she rushed back with small slices of cake and chocolate. She dashed in again and darted with a litre of multi-vitamin juice with two glasses.

'Baby,' she said, 'this is cake for you. Let's eat.' She took out a piece of it, bit it and put it into my mouth.

'Thanks.'

'No problem Baby. I love you,' she said filling the glasses. Markus snarled like it was in pains.

'Markus, Markus,' she said walking towards it.

'Please talk with it there. I hate dogs,' I said with a bad

face. She went and petted it for a while.

'Don't worry. It's our culture to pet animals.'

'I know. Animals are respected here than people like me.'

'Not all right. Children come first, the women follow, animals and then men like you come last,' she said laughing.

We finished eating the cake and she cleared the table.

'Baco, I wish we watch a film before bed.'

'No problem. Which one is the favourite?' She said nothing but searched. She found one and immediately switched off the light. The room was dark and the only light was dappling flashes from the bright television screen. Tina felt relaxed. Perhaps it was because of the fact that I never turned down her proposal. She threw her backside on my legs. I knew what would follow. A dry sent mixed with a strong perfume she wore caused my nostrils to wager.

'Your perfume is too much for my nose.'

'Sorry Baby,' she apologised. 'I will not wear it again.'

We watched the film for five minutes and she was like on heat. It was their common practice. From the sofa, we tumbled to the carpet and then rolled to under the dinning table, as she wailed in the greatest dazzling allure. Markus barked several times.

'Shot up your mouth, you dog,' I abused. She took my hand and we walked in the attire we were born into the bedroom. Really, it was a nonsense act. She did it several times per second. I had never jived in those guilty activities even with Nicoline that was the only thing in my life. The whole night was active. Even if she was barren, what I loaded in her waist could break the chains of barrenness. We discovered ourselves only when it was getting dawn. We were like weary soldiers who separated in a tough war and rejoined only after it had ended.

'Did you dream of me?' she asked in a feeble voice.

'Yes, I did. You're too appetising.' She was satisfied and feeling good.

'You have no job. How then do you have much money

to furnish your house?'

'I don't want to work,' she said. 'I have enough money in my account.'

'How comes that?'

'I benefited from my father. He passed away when I was still young. Before then, he had divorced my mother before his death. He was a business magnet and had willed all his property to my grandfather to hold for me.

'Wow, you must be a fortunate lady.'

'Thank God.'

'Where is your grandfather?'

'He lives in Essen, a town next to this.'

'What does he do there?'

'Nothing... He is old and handicapped. He was captured by the Russian soldiers at the age of eighteen during the Second World War after his leg was cut off by a machine gun.'

'What about your mother?'

'She too used to live there but she is of late. What of your own parents?'

'It's a sad story for the ears.'

'How sad is the story, Darling?'

I explained to her how an epidemic swept them away. She felt so depressed.

'Baby,' I said, 'I'm a sad man in my life.'

'Why?' she asked as she held me.

'I lost my parents and I've also made long in this country with no achievement. I yearn to meet my only sister back home. I think that will be my only source of comfort.' She looked into my eyes and saw sincerity. I climbed down the bed with wet eyes as if thinking the idea was a problem. I went to the bathroom. She sat in the sitting room weeping.

'Why are you in tears, Tina?' I asked.

'Where do you think I will go to? Why do you want to break my heart so soon?'

'It's not my fault,' I said. 'I'm an orphan and need to see

27

my only sister, Nicoline. I have the feeling for you but...'

She sat there thinking. I had a proposal to make but wasn't sure of her reactions. I was still to study certain points about her rectitude.

'It's time I make hay at the bright sun,' I thought as I looked at my face in a mirror preparing to leave.

'I'm on my way. See you any other day.' She looked at me with a demanding face and didn't respond. I walked out and she banged the door brutally. 'Fuck!' she said though I only heard the echoes. I went back to the camp with burning developments to share with Stoney.

'What's new, Baco the Lover Boy?' He was still in bed when I entered.

'Many things are in progress.'

'How is Fatima?' Fatima was a street jargon for a fat woman, though many girls in Germany at this time had the name.

'She's more beautiful and lovely this time,' I said. I have hooked her at a point and if God be my helper, something interesting will result.'

'What could be that?'

'She's home in painful sobs. I told her I am an orphan and that I will soon leave for home to see my only sister, Nicoline. She's afraid I'll dump her.'

Stoney never believed me. To him, I was not vibrant and elegant enough to cook such a story. But indeed, that was just the damn truth.

'If what you say is true, then you have shot the animal at the skull which is the right point. I mean you have directed the bullet into the ear drum of the elephant. Believe me, the large animal will fall.'

My mobile telephone rang.

'Who is that?' asked Stoney. 'Fatima,' I answered. He motioned his hand telling me not to pick up the call. The phone kept ringing. 'Now that she dies for you, show some disdain. Give an impression of no fascination of any kind.

Believe me, if you do this, she can hurriedly propose marriage or can undertake to bring Nicoline over. Better still, she can hurriedly take in.'

The phone kept ringing and vibrating at the same time. At the length of five minutes, it stopped and suddenly started ringing again. I dropped it on the table and we laughed at how someone was dying for another. Chinedu looked at me and shook his head. 'Why do you treat humans this way?' he asked compassionately.

'This is not maltreatment,' I replied. 'It's consolidating a step. You're still new here if really you are. By the time you make a year or two with no accomplishment, you might do more worst things than these. Can you recall the disaster their parents caused to our continent? Are you satisfied with history? From deceitful exploration to slavery, annexation, colonisation, re-colonisation, exploitation and even today, brain drain, human trafficking and sex slavery, are such terrible things one could never imagine. But those evil acts are real.'

'Forget about Chinedu,' added Stoney. 'His own tricks shall be worst from the way I see him. He resembles one who shall deal in drugs.'

Chinedu laughed and asked with a guilty face, 'Why do you say so?' Stoney flashed a sarcastic smile at him. 'Chinedu,' Stoney continued, 'You look like a radical who has made long in this country. Look at your hairstyle. It's not a common practice in Nigeria.'

'You've never been to my country before. How comes you know about hairstyles?'

'Even your ear lobes are perforated. This is a western crazy attitude. Any child with this kind of styles in any black African country is considered spoiled. It is an irritation to the community.'

As we talked, my mobile phone rang again. Tina Fatima was the one. I didn't whip it up. Rather, I danced at the *knick-knack* sound. Chinedu and Stoney laughed.

'You can pick it up now but be stern and get her the more upset,' Stoney said.

'Yes, hello,' I answered.

'Baby, why do you want to make the future strenuous?' I remained silent.

'Hi, Baby,' she emphasised, 'are you there?'

'Yes, Tina, I'm getting you. What's the matter? What's it that you couldn't tell me when I was there?' She was silent for some seconds and I could feel she was scared and careful.

'Baby, I wish to see and feel you. Can I pick you up?'

'I'm busy now. I'll find time to come.'

'No problem, Baby. I'll wait for you until evening.' Then I heard a long hiss as she kissed. I dropped the mobile and laughed. I slammed myself on the bed in gayness. Stoney applauded.

'If this kind of opportunity meets me, I have to play like a veteran of all times,' said Stoney. For hours, we sat discussing on strategies.

I left for Tina that evening. When I rang her bell, she never cared to know who was there. She opened. I entered and met her on the floor leaning backwards on the sofa. She was like a young woman who had just been tortured by untimely age. Her left hand supported her head while her right hand was on her knee.

'What's the matter,' I asked. She sighed like one who had cried the whole day and was still feeling the echoes, then starring at her toes.

'You asked me to come. If you don't feel like talking, let me go and leave you in peace.' She rose and sat on a table chair.

'Baco,' she said, 'why do you make things hard for me? Your behaviour towards me can push me to curse the day I was born.' She paused and wiped her wet nose.

'Baby,' she continued, 'tell me. Is it because you really want to see your sister or it's because I don't really appear good to you?'

'Tina, I love you and I can die for you. But I'm sorry to say if I don't see Nicoline, I can die an untimely death.'

'I can't understand you. So, this is how the love will end? We can make her fly over here.'

'I don't think she's going to appreciate the idea of coming to Europe though I've never asked her opinion on the issue.'

We were quiet for a couple of minutes. I maintained a serious solemn face. Within me, I was impressed. She held my hands tied. 'Baco, I love you,' she said. 'I prefer to make sacrifices for her coming than miss you. If it does not work, I'll follow you to Africa. Just look around and tell me a place for abandoned hearts. Tell me how people with broken hearts look like. For the sake of God, give me a chance to solve this matter. Your own contribution is just to give me *the go ahead*.'

'How do people with broken hearts look like?' I asked.

'They look sad,' she said. 'They are sad even in their dreams, turning such to nightmares. If you dump me, my life will be in ruins. Please, don't let me dream away my future. If really I fit your taste, give me the chance. I love you madly.'

I tried to imagine the dream she was out for, and I wondered why she was too stupid to think that I would make life with her. Well, the idea that women are frail when it comes to relationships came to me. Love could be funny. It could force even great Queens and Kings behave stupidly. Tina was no exception.

I appeared reluctant in all she was saying and still appeared as hopeless as a winter night. The love she had fumbled and dragged her live in was paining her like a fresh wound. Although I had said to her that she was beautiful, she knew it that she wasn't the marketable type. Making long there would mean reconciling with her. Thus, I told her 'I want to go. I have to do something back home with Stoney.'

'Please can I see Stoney?'

'Not today,' I said. 'I think he's busy.'

A thought rushed my mind. I could guess why she

wanted to see him. However, I thought, it was working on my own advantage. She knew I was close to Stoney and she would know many things about me if close to him too.

'Please, just tell him I would like to see him for a talk,' she said.

Stoney was wise and would always give good advice. When I reached the camp that day, he was so excited when I told him about the pressure from Tina. He accepted to meet her.

'I just have to tell her we have a small problem and that I don't so much get involved in your issues. Then, I have to propose what she can do.' Stoney said.

'If it works and Nicoline comes, you deserve something so special,' I said. For Nicoline to come over would cost me lots of money which I never had. The situation then was penurious but God was making a way, I thought.

We planned for them to meet in two days. It was like two years for her. She would ring my mobile phone even in dreams. Each time the phone rang, we would say in chorus, 'Fatima.'

Summer had reached its peak. It was time lovers were exposing themselves to the comfort of the sun in tiny pants, a thing most African would never do. On sand on the streets or on small fields too, some were naked, kissing their lovers. At the sight of a naked person in an African society, people would surely consult the Gods pleading for forgiveness. When such behaviours persisted, traditional prayer warriors would set in.

Some people took it to mean a curse to see the nakedness of a woman.

Summer was equally a moment when most people were leaving for other nations to enjoy themselves. Some left for countries within Europe, while others left for Africa to enjoy a natural environment. That is, an environment most of them yearned to have but which never would come back to them. Theirs was a permanently cemented one. No natural ground and flowers. It was the reason some of them went for their second time and never returned.

In fact, summer was a moment of hope but it was a radically tough moment for Tina.

More, it was Monday the week that Stoney was supposed to start depositing documents for his marriage with Margeret Bucker. Indeed, it was a hectic period.

Stoney rang Tina's mobile. 'You said you want to see me today. Are you free now?'

'I'm free Stoney. If you can come, you make my week a good one. Please, I need you now madly.'

Stoney immediately left for Tina while I waited home for feedbacks. He rang just once and Tina opened. She was weeping when Stoney entered.

'Why are you in tears?' Stoney asked.

'I am getting disappointed. What Baco wants to do, I can't understand.'

'What then is the matter Tina?' For a while, she couldn't explain. In some serious echoes of pain, she heaved a sigh and shook her head.

'Stoney,' she said, 'the only hill where I just buried my heart is sinking. I am getting frustrated.'

'Explain what you are talking about.'

'I mean Baco wants to leave for home. Has he told you that?' She muttered in tears as if *leave for home* would finish her life. She explained wiping her eyes with her hands.

'Tina, we're having some misapprehensions with Baco. I hardly get involved in his confidential affairs. However, I know he yearns to see an only sister.'

'What do you think could be the solution to this matter? I don't want to miss him.'

'Lady, understand that I'm not supposed to involve in this matter. Just of recent, Baco started behaving strange to me. I thought it's because of much affection for you but now it's as if he wants to leave you. To be as candid as a mirror, I doubt what is confusing him. I don't know what to say.'

'Do you know of Nicoline?'

'For that, I do but not much,' answered Stoney.

'What little? Just tell me please.'

'I know she is beautiful and is the lone sister. I equally know that he wishes to have another moment of comfort with her. He is really curious about that. That is what I knew but at moment, I can't really tell.'

Tina continued to weep. For some thirty minutes, they didn't communicate with each other. She was as hopeless as one facing a firing squad.

'Please, for my sake,' she said, 'just forget whatever differences you have with Baco and tell me what to do. My life is rushing towards an unknown destination and I don't just know what to do. I'm just getting confused and frustrated.'

'Why do you get yourself in this kind of situation? You're a gorgeous young woman. Why can't you look for another friend?'

'Stoney,' she said, 'if I don't face this challenge, I will live to be challenged. It's not that Baco is not affectionate. I know he truly loves me but for the fact that he wants to see his sister. Reason with me too. What if I look for another man without this kind of problem but who doesn't love me?'

'Yes, lady, that could be a sure fact. Yet, understand that life is sometimes paradoxical. There is no Mr. or Mrs *Perfect*. It is for you to... I mean that is...' Stoney fumbled with his lips.

'I can't understand you Stoney,' she said.

'Alright you are now squeezing words from my jaws,' Stoney relaxed. 'What I have to suggest now should never get to Baco, otherwise, you mar the whole relationship. I think the best thing for you to do is to embark on a radical step to bring Nicoline here. Sometimes, it is not safe back home because the social life of the indigenes doesn't march with that of strangers. You could be equally exposed to more danger which I don't just want to mention.'

'Oh God!' she rejoined, 'May you work things out for

me.' She sighed painfully and said, 'It's not long since I started believing in God but what I know is that angels are spirits of God that could be manifested through normal human beings like you. Something is telling me you're the right person God has sent to efface my afflictions. Please, don't be hurt. How is it possible to bring Nicoline soonest?'

'It's a question of money. You just need to send an invitation letter and in the course of that, prove that you can finance the trip and provide for accommodation. You should know this better. My only doubt now is how strong you are financially.'

'Don't beat your brain about that. I need a family to enjoy what was willed to me.'

'Well, if that be the case, things can work out effortlessly. The only problem is that Baco is a man with the highest ego I've ever met in my life. That's a weak point I have noticed in him. If you're really out to see this dream come a reality, you have to keep him comforted. Just get some cash from your account any of these days and give him to send home on your behalf. That would surely ease your conversation by phone with his sister, in case you want to introduce the chapter to her. She too does not want to stoop low to certain issues. She is not the type that yearns for the west like others.'

Tina heaved, walked to the cupboard and took out a bottle of champagne with two flutes.

'Do you like champagne?' she asked.

'I do in occasions like this. Otherwise, I would have preferred some fruit juice,' Stoney responded. She filled the two champagne flutes though still with a desperate face. She was still wondering. For several minutes, there was dead silence. The only thing that was in motion was the pendulum and the second hand of a grandfather clock.

'This clock appears grandiose,' said Stoney pointing to it.

'Really,' she said, 'it's a gift from my late father. He used to have complicated and luxurious things.'

'He must have been so rich in his days.'

'Of course,' she said. 'My great grandfather came from the Netherlands. He used to be a chief slave trader in those old days. That is why he had the opportunity to accumulate lots of wealth.'

'You mean to say you're enjoying money from the sale of humans,' Stoney said jokingly.

'It sounds funny but that's the veracity,' she said. 'We're not to be blamed. We grew up and were too fortunate to meet accumulated wealth.'

'If the gods of the African jungle decide to blow their trumpets for the past disaster, it would be a catastrophic tragedy.'

'What do you mean, Stoney?'

'I mean, if people were to look back to the past suffering of humankind, the black forest would surely breathe a lethal tongue of fire.' Tina smiled in doubts.

'Your discussion seems scary. You don't have to take us to the past, though I know that what our parents did in those days deserves returns.'

'That's not even what we're asking for. What we yearn for is just our freedom. Our people need to move freely in this world, be left to control their own economies and to munch a little from the international cake which they've laboured for. We're not free even in our own continent. The remote control of Africa is in the west. Things like cocoa and coffee come from Africa, but about eighty percent of Africans don't know the taste of that. It is sold abroad cheaper than in our continent.'

'No, Baco. For that, your prefects are to be blamed.'

'That's not true. Their minds are controlled by the west.'

'How is that done?'

'Most of them have their money in western banks and if they don't abide to what is needed, the money is confiscated. Some of our leaders too have constructed most expensive business centres here like hospitals and schools. They fear to lose these things and for that reason, they do what is not of the people but what is technically of the west. I know you're a young lady and might not understand these things.'

'I do but at my own level. My only doubt is why your elders have to leave their wills drawn by strangers. This still makes me blame them. Look at how you people are suffering in the world.'

'That's why I say you're still too young in mind to understand. The people were open to early strangers and unaware of what was behind the visits. Until now, it is their culture to be of good hospitality. They only found themselves raped in chains when it was too late... But it counts to the advantages of people like you. If people don't have to travel for better leaving conditions, you won't have met people like Baco.'

Tina smiled and looked at Stoney as if her mind reflected what she had been crying for. Then she repeated the name twice, 'Baco, Baco. I love that boy so much that I can offer to sell my heart just to buy the love.' She was relaxed. 'I wish we conclude this issue of Nicoline, because there are only two things now. Either I bring her here and maintain my relationship with Baco or I take away my life if Baco abandons me. It's not easy to have a boy like him who loves.'

'I don't expect such words from you. Only cowards do kill themselves.'

'What am I if I can't have someone I yearn for? I prefer to spend all I have than let him go. That's the only thing I value in my life now.'

'I don't know what to say. You're the sole dancer at the arena. Just follow the rhythm the way you hear it. You should avoid as much as possible to let Baco know what we have discussed here today. Just believe in miracles and it shall happen.'

'Well, let's just hope so.'

Stoney never made long again with Tina. He left for the camp. She remained back thinking painfully.

'How bad it is in life to see and later be blind!' She

37

thought. 'Better to be born a blind person. Better never to taste a favourite food than taste and never part take of it. Life is hard. I have no mother and no father. God, have pity and give this boy to me... Death too is hard... I would have kissed a goodbye to the world than remain in pains. If husbands could be on auction sale like goods, I would have been the highest *bidder* of Baco. What a paradox in life that our white brothers are rushing for the black girls while the black boys are rushing for the white girls. Baco should have been dying for me as black boys are rushing for white women. How ironical that a fish yearns for water while it swims in it! Maybe it is because I'm not a slim model like other girls... But he swears he loves me but for...'

Chapter Four

Until the following week, Tina remained in serious thoughts and pains. I made it tough for her to start the topic of bringing Nicoline to Europe. I bounced the phone on her on several occasions.

'I think it's enough,' said Stoney to me one day. 'Just call her for a drink one of these days and give in for her idea. But let her know that you don't really cherish it.'

'Of course, Stoney,' I said. 'I have to compel her give me the money even triple. After all, that is just a pinch of what they stole and are still draining from Africa. The more, I don't have any love for her and I careless to put her bankrupt.'

'My top nigger,' said Stoney in great happiness, 'let's just hope that this year will be a successful one for our residence permits.'

'I have to let Nicoline know of the deal. Nobody knows what would happen if she is not aware.'

'She has to understand and should be happy for God answering her prayers.'

'We have to start thinking of how to manage the matter when she comes.'

'Not really now. We don't need to start calculating steps up the hill when we are still kilometres away from it. You don't border. Just let her come first and the solutions will come even in surplus.'

I dialled her number. 'Baby,' she cried. 'This is a serious issue. It's not only the matter of your sister coming here. I also love you so much. I miss you and I wish to see you here so that we can talk it out together. Why do you dump me for several days?'

'I told you I have my own worries in this country. You're not supposed to ask me this rubbish on phone,' I brutalised.

'Alright, I never meant it to hurt you,' she pampered. 'When and how can we have a talk?'

'Today, if possible. You can call later to know whether

I'll come or not.'

'Thanks, my sweetheart. I'll do just that. I love you, baby.' I clicked off my phone while she was still on. There was frustration. She was prepared to apologise even for mistakes never done just to please me.

We talked about the issue in the camp with Stoney the whole time and were getting fade up.

'Switch on the TV. I am getting bored,' Stoney pleaded. When I switched it on and flipped to an international channel, the topic on discussion was *identity crises*. The crew on stage included journalists, a French, an Irish, an American, a Dutch, some Germans who were linked up from other channels to share their opinions. There were arguments on how children with parents from different races were becoming more in number than real children of the country.

'The worst thing is that some of these mixed race children don't know one of the parents,' said Stoney.

'Of course, some people abandon their kids because after they were born, no residence permit was given them. If I have a child with Tina and they refuse to grant me a stay, I just have to abandon the thing and go my way.'

'That's most dangerous,' said Stoney. 'A child who does not know one of his or her parents lacks moral upbringing. They are like walls of a house found on mud or dust. At maturity, they think that they have lost the most important part of their lives and see no reason to be respectful.'

There was a knock at the door. It was Chinedu.

'Come in Nigger,' said Stoney.

'What's up men?' he said in return.

'Get away!' Do you think we're here in the States where English language is taking a strange shape?' I said.

'It's a weird but good shape,' he fired back laughing. 'If you can speak like an American, with perforated loops, and plated hair, you will surely have one of these bitches around. They love such crazy things.'

'Somehow, you're right,' said Stoney. 'If we are like those

40

rogues, we would have had a stay long time. If you continue at this pace, you will have a German lady so fast. The more so, you are tall and muscular. They don't care about too much handsomeness.' Chinedu smiled and looked at Baco. 'What of Baco? He's not tall but has Tina.'

'You're not only tall but muscular. Baco's case is one amongst the few exceptions. You equally appear like one who can easily pass their test: that is to lick them all over their bodies and do something so that they feel their heads. That is what they want. Even if your nose is as big as that of the hippopotamus, or your face as rough as the back of a tortoise, once you have enormous muscles, you will have a girl.'

Chinedu was a good fan to such issues. He sighed and said, 'My guys, I desperately need a lady no matter how ugly she is. I need a stay in this country as fast as possible.'

'Are you prepared to lick?' asked Stoney.

'I've been licking without any pay. If I should lick now with the hope of having a German stay, I think I should do it with the dexterity of a dog over a sweet bone.' We laughed as he thrust his tongue in the air like rehearsing.

It was not too long when Tina called again. I almost rejected the call. 'Just pick the call,' Stoney said. I did but answered her sluggishly as I said, 'I'll be there in about half an hour.'

Through chocked terraces, I walked slowly towards Kama Street.

'What kind of life is this?' I thought on the way. 'There is completely no respect of integrity, no maintenance of grace. Across the mountains into the legs of foolish ladies has become the new order. Can one really account for all these things? It's a complete waste and abuse of divine resources.' Those thoughts pained me like a bad tooth.

I rang Tina's bell. She opened. I met her as wimpy as a weary soldier just from a battle. At length, she could not talk. I balanced myself on the sofa and soon, I was asleep. When I got up, I only discovered her snoring on my lapse. I woke her.

'How are you doing?' I asked and she never answered but rather starred at me for several seconds and then said, 'Baco, I don't only love you. I need you. Look at me. I'm a changed girl just for the few days you've abandoned and starved me. For the sake of God, please, develop love for humans like me.'

'How can I do that?'

'Please, allow me bring your sister and that's the solution. I don't care how much that could cost me.'

When she said that, she kept looking into my eyes and moving her hand up and down my chest. Then, she leaned on me with her front side.

'Don't bother. I have given you the *go ahead*. You can bring her if it pleases you.'

Her eyes fell. She gripped my lips with hers and we fell rolling on the ground from one side to the other. There on the floor, we went three full rounds. I was exhausted and thirsty.

'Please, can I have some fruit juice?'

'Of course,' she answered rushing to the fridge for it. I emptied three glasses as she kept looking and admiring me.

'I will meet my grandfather on Monday to prepare an invitation letter for your sister,' she said.

'Are you sure he is going to do it?'

'Of course,' she said. 'I would have done it but for the fact that I don't have a bigger apartment. He wants me to enjoy my inherited property. He always asks me this kind of opportunities.'

'Well, do it the way you feel best. I have to prolong my stay on that same Monday. So you have to go do it alone.'

I was never happy when it came to the issue of extending residence permits. Just for the short time being with her, she was able to realise it.

'I bought something that you like so much. Guess what,' said Tina smiling.

42

'Tell me. I can't say.'

'I have bought 'Reggae CDs for you. I think you will like them.' She took out one of them and slotted to play.

'*...emancipate yourselves from mental slavery,*
None but ourselves can free our own minds...'

'Do you know that redeeming voice?' I asked her.

'That's Bob,' she said looking at the picture of Bob Marley.

'So you too have to emancipate yourself from this society's mental enslavement, never thinking of any stress anymore.'

'You've said just the truth. Individuals have to yank themselves from the deep precipice. The mushroom international organisations have all failed. Humankind remains in deep shit and pains.'

'Of course,' she replied, 'you people risk repatriation. You have to make up your mind now. We can even get married now so that you don't fall victim to deportation.'

'See how you reason stupidly this time. Do you want me to engage because of affections or because I fear repatriation?'

'Baco, I love you and believe that you too love me. Getting married will surely amplify our relationship and also lessen the load placed on your head by the government.'

Chapter Five

It was Monday morning and the people had resumed work after the weekend. I had decided to make the night at Tina's. I was exhausted and broken on her bed. She kissed me again as she was ready to leave for hospital before going to her grandfather. She had complained the previous day of light fever.

'You have to go for your visa, right?' She asked.

'Exactly,' I responded. 'I will only see you in the evening when back from the foreign office.'

'It's all right, baby. I love you so much,' she said, kissed me and took off. I heard the car negotiating out from down the building. I rose from bed and had a bath to gain some strength. Within thirty minutes, I approached the bus stop. A bus passed by and idled there. I ran fast for about two hundred metres to jump in. I was breathing out all air in me. As I was almost to touch it, the driver kicked off after about three passengers dropped. It was unfortunate. I shouted, 'wicked man!' Passengers at the back of the bus looked at me laughing as they saw me holding my knees to gain strength. I stood there waiting for another bus ready to leave for the foreign office. A long white bus of about thirty seats idled at the stop. I climbed in and bought a ticket from the bus driver. As it kicked off, I walked inside looking for a comfortable seat. There were some free seats. I walked to the last roll of four seats. There, a white lady sat. I sat just close to her.

'Hallo,' I greeted with a smile. She looked at me and turned her face. 'How are you?' I greeted again. She looked at me with great disappointment, then stood and walked to the front and sat amongst two other ladies. They all turned and laughed at me provocatively. She was cute and of average age.

The bus soon idled at a stop and more than ten passengers dropped and some more people too jumped in. There were no more empty seats in front. Four other ladies walked to the back as they just entered. I moved my damn ass to the last seat of the roll where I was, just to allow them sit. They immediately turned off towards the middle of the bus where they stood until two stops and dropped. As the bus kicked off again, they looked at me with bitter faces from outside. One of them raised her upper lip to stop air from getting into her nostrils. That act was to let me know that I smelled. The bus was at the last stop and I descended.

In front of the foreign office were many other people queuing for visas. I joined the single long line and gradually, we push-walked forward.

The foreign office was a building of many rooms. Some were for establishment of work permits, visa renewal and others were for interrogations by foreign office police. There waiting were Arabs, blacks, and other white skin people. People were entering into, and coming out of the office. It was my turn to enter the main door and then to make way to room ten for a visa. In there was Frau Lisa, Herr Silber, Mathäus and some few others who I never succeeded pronouncing their names. Herr Silber was one too rare in smiles. He was tall and of great enigma.

'Guten tag,' I greeted them. 'Tag,' replied Silber.

'I wish to renew my residence permit,' I said. He took the white piece of paper and perused it as if something was wrong. I saw some stars in his eyes sparking strangely. I was heavily dreaded. He rose and looked at me again. His colleagues were busy with some paper work.

'Herr Baco,' he said, 'we have to delve a little into your case before renewing your visa. Understood?'

'Yes, Sir,' I responded.

'Then you can stand out,' he said walking towards the main office with the vigour of a patriotic soldier at the verge of a war. At an alley, there stood others waiting.

'Hello,' greeted a Nigerian.

'Hi. How are you doing?' I greeted back.

'Are you waiting for a visa?'

'If not, why should I be standing here?'

'How many months do they usually give you?'

'Some times, they stamp one month and some other times three weeks on my *Duldung*. Duldung simply meant *temporary residence permit*.

'That's bad,' he said. 'So you have to come here all the time. The authorities in our Division give us six months though they give us little money for food stuff.'

'That's the big disadvantage with a federal system. Each state has its own independent laws. Applicants from the same country with the same case face different treatments. Racists find it easy to exercise their bad attitudes.'

'Of course, federalism is bad,' he said. 'It finds it difficult to reconcile its internal rules and regulations vis-à-vis international agreements.'

'My brother, the earlier our country is delivered from the mess, the better so that we can return. I've found no justice in this present world.'

As we discussed, Silber suddenly walked out of the main office followed by the chief officer.

'Mr. Baco, please come to the main office,' he said and they fell back into the office and I followed. In the main office, was a tall man manipulating the computer and answering a telephone call at the same time. For some time, none of them talked to me. Rather, Silber keyed the door and asked me to sit. I was dumbstruck when told me, 'Your case has ended and has been completely rejected. Now we're sending you back to your country of origin.'

Silber looked at me again and turned to the Chief who was seriously flipping papers in a file.

'Huh,' sighed the chief officer, 'we're sorry. You're under arrest. We have to take you now to a judge. There, before him, we'll make an oral application for your detention at a deportation camp. While in detention, we will collaborate with your country embassy to get documents to push you back home.'

That kick could pull my teeth. A chill ran down my spine

as those words pierced my heart. I couldn't take to my heels. The situation was as that of a fly corked in a bottle. He keyed the door.

'Hey, young man,' said Silber taking out handcuffs from his pockets. 'I am a policeman and we have the right to arrest you.'

Two other huge officers darted from another inner room looking smart with great muscles. One of them took the handcuffs from him and forced my hands backwards. They took my handset and put it off. Through the back door, they forced me into a police car. Those who were on the line never knew what was happening to me inside. Silber handled the steering with the dexterity of a motor racer. He soon negotiated a corner towards a court building. They tugged me from the hairs and pushed me into an office. I could guess it was the office of the judge. On a table with many files, was the picture of an old judge with a frightful wig. At a corner was a man like a secretary near a computer. Silber called in a warder who had been waiting. The judge too entered followed by an interpreter. They all took their various positions.

'Herr Baco,' said the translator, 'my name is Wolfman. I'm a translator. This is Justice Finger and this one here is a warder who will take you to the deportation prison after this court session. This is a secretary. He will type whatever thing you say.'

The judge coughed a little to clear his throat and flipped some pages in a file, then asked, 'What's your name?'

'I can't answer this question,' I said as he was flipping more papers in a file. This was a great annoyance to them and at this time they decided to type their judgment.

I was to be in detention for a maximum period of three months during which the authorities would find means of repatriation.

'Please,' said the judge, 'you're obliged to sign this judgement. You have a period of three months to appeal if you feel cheated or abused.'

'I wish to inform my lawyer that I am in this situation. I would also like to call my wife to let her know this.'

'Are you officially married according to the basic matrimonial rules and regulations of this country?' asked the judge.

'No, Sir.'

'Then I'm sorry, you fall short of the right to make a call. You have just one option. That is to appeal while at the deportation camp if you wish.'

I was not myself. In that bitterness, I said harshly, 'Is this not an abuse of right? I must call my lawyer or girlfriend.'

'You talked of a wife and now you are talking of girlfriend. Very soon, you will talk of a father. Let it be an abuse of right. You are now under incarceration.'

Like a swallow, Silber swooped on me. I remained in handcuffs. He dragged me backwards from the handcuffs.

'Is this the western life?' I thought. I have never felt such a humiliation in my country and entire life. They squeezed me again into the same police car. It kicked off towards the main road. It soon entered an artificial forest through a tiny road with wild flowers. The further we went the narrower and gloomy the road became. Some strong feeling of sadness and pain lurked the whole environment. For several minutes, Silber kept tearing the gloomy path while discussing with the warder.

We arrived at the camp of five structures. There was a metal gate. Soon, the first gate automatically opened. Other officers came and took me out of the car. They opened six other gates one after the other and took me to the prison office. Silber was off with the car. There in the office were some long time prisoners helping the officers. They would help take a new prisoner's clothes and to bring for him prison dresses. There were many warders and wardresses going in and out of the various offices with files. I was in a different world though at first sight, I couldn't concur with my eyes.

A wall of about ten metres kept the camp closed. Even an acrobatic vampire could not make his way out. From one structure to the other was a distance of about twenty metres. One of them was a four-storey structure. Each of them contained about four hundred rooms. From this line of structures to the sport arena was a metal fence with barbwires. In one of the buildings was a room meant for some medical services.

'Take off all you have on,' said the chief. 'We have to give you new prison clothes.' He called the old inmates and they brought an old blue jeans trouser, an extra large T-shirt, one old towel, a pant, a pair of old shoes, a pullover, toothbrush and a tablet of soap. The chief starred at me with bad eyes.

'I've said you should take off all the rags you have on,' he groaned.

'Where is the dressing room?' I asked.

'No privacy in this prison, nor is there any right of choice,' he replied heaving backwards in astonishment.

'I was told this is a camp and not a prison. What's my crime?'

'Your presence here is a crime if you don't know,' said the warder. A lady with a heavy tummy darted from another room and called for the prison security officers to tear off my dresses if I hesitated. I had to bow to them as I took off all I had and stood natural. The chief looked at my black thing and flashed a sarcastic smile. It irritated me. I looked at him and asked, 'What's humorous?'

'Your thing must have wallowed between female thighs several times,' he responded laughing while supporting his head with his hands. His face suddenly changed dark.

'Take away those rags,' he said to the boys and asked me to dress up with the prison clothes.

'Sir,' I complained, 'this is not my size of shoes.' He called for the lady with a large stomach. 'Come with another pair of shoes for this young man.' She lackadaisically walked in and brought out another pair of shoes, then threw them on the ground for me to pick saying, 'Do you have this in your country? You have the effrontery to make a choice. Idiot.'

'You Satan,' I fired back though she never got me as she banged the door after her. The two prisoners walked towards the waiting room and looked at me. They all motioned their tombs in the air in appreciation of my words.

The chief asked, 'Do you want to tell any of your people that you are here?'

'Of course, I desperately do.'

'Come then,' he said adjusting the telephone for me. I dialled Tina.

'Tina... Hallo.'

'It's me Baco.'

'Hey, Schatz,' she fumbled, 'I have just returned from my grandfather.'

'Tina, I've been arrested. I'm now at the deportation prison.'

'Shit,' she screamed. 'What a fuck! What happened to you, darling?' I could not answer as the man said, 'Stop it is more than two minutes.' He took the phone from me and hocked it off. The lady suddenly re-entered and he said to her 'Take him to room 15 block one. There are four other blacks there.'

From the Chief's office to block one were about six gates. Each block was separated from the other by a double metal barrier as high as the building itself. She opened one gate after the other from block four to one, walked to room fifteen and opened the heavy door. In there were four boys- David Wills from Liberia, Lionel from Benin Republic, Akeh from Togo and Okonkwo from Nigeria.

'Here are your African brothers,' she said. 'You have to make some time here while the government will try for papers in collaboration with your country embassy to send you back.' She pushed me into the room and closed the door. As she banged the door forcefully, the noise from it bombed my ears. The inmates laughed at me as I trembled.

'Welcome to hell,' greeted David Willis from his small bunk bed. I remained quiet and motionless.

They showed me a bunk bed at the top. In the small square room was a small table at the centre, a television and a toilet near the door. There was an old shrank for keeping dresses though it was almost empty.

'Why is the door keyed while we remain in?' I asked after about an hour.

'It makes the difference from when you are in the city and when you are in prison,' replied Akey. When I asked them whether there were chances for release, Akey said, 'You can only get released if you have a baby here or when married.'

'I have a girlfriend but no baby,' I replied.

'For me it is even better to go die in my country and be buried there than die here. If you die here, they have to grind the remains and blow the dust off,' Lionel said. At first, I thought he was saying so out of despair, but I came to realise the fact.

'Those are the consequences of being a refugee. I've been here now for nine months. They've not deported nor released me,' said David Willis. When I heard the word, *nine months*, a shock rumbled my heart.

'Nine months in this state of affairs?' I questioned in bewilderment.

'Yes,' said Lionel, 'here, it's possible to make long as well as be pushed back in a few days. That's why you can hear many people talking abnormally. Worst of it all, when one is mentally upset, he is sent to the basement.' Others shook their heads in confirmation. As they explained, some one opened the door.

'Who is Baco?' he asked.

'I am, Sir.' Then he said to me, 'I am in charge of this block. In case of any questions, you can contact me. My name is Woods Rocks, a security officer.' Then he handed me a paper containing rules and regulations of the camp.

'In breach of any of these rules,' he said, 'you will be sent to make two weeks in the cellar.' Then after, he brutally banged the door. At the back page of the paper, was a schedule for breakfast, lunch, and the permanent two kinds of food that would be available. There were also basic rights of man on the paper. I perused it. There would be one hour for break after working in the cellar daily. There was thirty minutes for Sports and all these were daily except Saturdays and Sundays.

From four to five was relaxing hour. Some days too, there were sporting activities from five until six pm. During sports, inmates would be doing weight lifting, play football or table tennis in a small keyed hall. At the end of every sports hour, inmates were to be in their various rooms locked.

On Saturdays was an hour for Church services rendered by a visiting pastor though there was a permanent pastor who the prisoners never loved.

In every room was a speaker for passing general information. They would shout from their office passing the same information to all the rooms like commanders in a military camp. Through the same speakers, one could receive a particular radio station chosen from the main office. Inmates would work in the cellar from the hours of 7 am to 4 pm.

It was 4 pm. 'It's time for you to relax outside,' said a voice from the speaker. It was the first time I was hearing that. They opened the doors.

Many security officers stood at the corridors waiting for inmates to go out. We soon packed full the corridors waiting. We were soon at a small grassy arena with wooden benches. I was still to familiarise myself with the new environment. Naivety was still on my face, though I had started gathering some bravery like a cock in a strange environment.

There were people from many other countries. Some greeted me. Some others were walking hopelessly round the small place. Many were in deepest soliloquy. Some squatted on the field reading novels. A tall man passed by. He looked at me strangely. I greeted him.

'How are you called,' he greeted back and asked.

'I'm Baco from Cameroon.'

'Sad to meet you in this heaven,' he said smiling though I was not stable in mind.

'I'm Tita from Cameroon too.'

'What a coincidence,' I said relaxed and moving my buttocks for him to sit.

'How long are you here?'

'Five months. The embassy has not established travel documents for my repatriation. I'm praying that they release me one of these days... Do they have any document from you?'

'No, I've never given them any identification paper. I doubt whether our embassy can sign for my repatriation without a paper to prove that I am a Cameroonian.'

'Not possible. Our embassy needs some paper confirmation. That's why the authorities want to establish a kangaroo office to be able to identify us as Cameroonians and to repatriate us.'

'How can that happen?' I asked.

'It will and it's possible. The office in Cologne already exists. Some white men who have stayed in Cameroon for long in collaboration with some Cameroonians here are working seriously on that.'

'You mean our own brothers?'

'Of course, if they can save the small money given them why can't they do it?'

'What then will the embassy say to that kind of office?'

'Baco,' Tita explained, 'maybe you can't understand today's mafia. The vagabond leaders back home want to die in power and they have declared themselves as the indomitable and infallible *kingkongs* of Cameroon. They sit and sign anything they want.'

'One needs to take his will from the hands of man and submit it into the hands of God. Just imagine. Our situation is like that of a rat mole that escapes from water in its hole only to climb up a tree of wild ants. It's only here one realises that back home would have been manageable.'

Tita shook his head in disappointment when he saw one security officer passing. Then he said, 'I will have what I deserve in that land and this animal treatment will be history.'

'My only fear is that they should not behave the Iyadema, or the Kabila way.'

'What do you mean?' he asked.

'I mean to be president in our continent nowadays is hereditary. The son would likely be like father. Our case can be more easy because there will be support from above. Our former masters can support that.'

'Obviously, any humble child would always have father's support.'

People were walking round as we discussed. Some stood in small groups of about three or four. Some were standing single deep in reflection. In all, there was demarcated freedom mingled with pain, despair and greatest dissatisfaction.

One security officer saw us from the other end of the field. We were almost like feeling free as we talked about home issues. A nostalgic thought was already moving down my mind. The security man dropped the half cigarette he was smoking and walked threateningly towards us. He stopped and looked directly at us but Tita pretended as if the officer was unheeded.

'What are you people talking about feeling so relaxed?' asked the officer, Woods Rocks.

'And what do you want us to talk about,' Tita shot back.

'Talk about your return to your homes, idiot.'

'Why not talk about you licking a lady's anus,' Tita fired back with anger but Woods never heard as he whipped his Walki Talki from his khaki trousers to answer a call. As he talked, he walked away from us. When he dropped the call, he walked to another group of inmates who were in a small debate. In the group were people from Iraq, Syria, Russia, Morocco, Lebanon and others. He listened and we saw him laughed.

'Look at that coffee brown teeth man. Why is he laughing?' Tita abused.

'Maybe he wants to stop them from talking,' I said.

'No, he knows where to talk. Those are the people who can easily flog him up.'

'Not even that. It's a crime for us to be born. Our presence on the planet earth is a nuisance. It seems that a black man suffers wherever he goes.'

'That's why I say there is no true justice in the world,' said Tita

'People behave worse than animals. Many things are becoming possible nowadays but for humans to recognise humans will be an issue of centuries to come.'

The idea that I was in a strange and hopeless place suddenly splashed my mind. My whole body quaked. Then I thought aloud forgetting that Tita was hearing me, 'Where really am I?'

'Just where we have ever yearned at home to be,' said Tita yawning and laughing at the same time. I realised myself in that thought. I was desperate and frustrated though I kept saying, 'God don't fail to remember me.'

'Well,' said Tita frustratingly, 'they have tried in helping. We are the unfortunate ones.'

The security officer shouted, 'Ten more minutes, it will be break over,' as if we were in an academic institution.

'Are there other Cameroonians here?'

'Of course,' he replied. They are all over the other building with other Africans. They will have their own free hour later but by that time we'll be in our rooms.' Then I asked whether he was current with the events back home. He told me many ministers were behind bars for mismanagement. He said the Police caught one of the ministers escaping to Gabon with a colossal sum of money.

The security officer commanded and we started walking towards our rooms through the tiny passageway.

Camp life had begun. Freedom was as scarce and precious to me like a piece of gold in a western land. It was even an almost none existing stuff. A thing I immediately started yearning for madly. The only right then was to post a letter. I thought of Tina and my lawyer.

There was rice and some white soup we met on the table when we retired from break. The whitish soup was as pure water poured into blinded Irish potatoes. If I ate that one, it would drain my blood, I thought. My mates tried first but could not finish it.

'Is this what you eat daily or today is just an unfortunate day?' I asked.

'We would have been too better up if the food has always been like this,' said Lionel flipping television channels.

'Then I have to invite my girlfriend here. I have two things now in mind; either I am freed immediately or deported. I can't hug this for goodness sake.'

'It's a different world here, Baco,' said Akeh. 'From this forest you see to the nearest town is forty five kilometres. If something happens here, it does so with no knowledge of the press. Even if you want to shout, nobody will ever hear you. It's only God Almighty who can rescue us from this rut.'

One could not hear the sound of a car, nor was there any noise from any domestic animal. The only noise was that from the inmates. There was no highway nearby. We were like a crew in space. We were like victims in the deepest and most secret dungeon. It was worse than a nightmare. There was an evil force chasing my peace. That was a force in full speed after me though I couldn't see. The environment was so silent and sorrowful so much that even domestic birds seemed scared. It was like the life of an insect during unfavourable conditions so much that it sealed its shell, and the only activity was to think within itself. It was a horrible thing indeed! I asked for a piece of paper and wrote to Tina, how she could reach the camp.

Chapter Six

Hours were rushing and so too the days. Monday was gone, Tuesday, and it was Thursday. It was afternoon and a security officer opened our small room and said to me, 'One Tina wants to see you. Do you know her?'

'Yes, Sir,' I eagerly responded. 'She's my wife to be.' Woods smiled astonished and egregious wrinkles immediately wired his face.

'So you hope to get married?' he asked looking into my eyes.

Lionel looked at him. He had been there for long and could understand Woods better.

'Why all these fucking words to this gentleman?' asked Lionel. 'Is it because he's new? I'm a good man to fuck your stinking ass. Do you have any right to ask questions to a deportee?' Woods wasn't at ease then.

One story of camp life had it that some crazy inmates brutalised and strangulated a security officer. It happened when Woods was new there. Thus making a long time in a particular room and exchanging hash words with prisoners was risky. Woods walked out and I followed him to the visiting hall. There were four metal gates like doors to reach the visiting room. We passed through an underground tunnel, then into a hall. Except one looked through a small window, night and day could not be distinguished.

From the last gate, I saw Tina on a table chair desperately waiting. What was I going to tell her? Was it how much love I had for her or how I would marry her? I was frustrated in ideas as she stood as the only hope.

Tina held me with her right hand supporting her head with the left.

'Baco,' she cried, 'what's happening to us? Is it temptation or the test of God?'

It was strange hearing such words from Tina. If she

59

could mention God, then the wheel of good hope was turning. To read a Bible page or pray was a waste of time to her.

'Since when have you started calling the name of God?' I asked but she never spoke a word. Her eyes sweated tears. At length, we held eyes in perplexity. Her own were mingled with love. I could see it clearly. She squeezed her eyes with her fingers and said, 'Baco, I'm pregnant.'

An undefined spirit sprang from my heart into my brain and at same time started sinking down to my system.

My head fell on the table but she raised it up and starred into my eyes. 'Please, darling, don't disappoint me,' she said. 'I will work hard with your lawyer for your release.'

'Release? No. I will be taken to the embassy tomorrow. If possible, the Ambassador will issue travel documents for me to go back. The future is dark and marshy. I don't want to disappoint you but your country wants to do so.' She looked at me with highest speculation. I could see she was painfully thinking.

'My grandfather issued an invitation letter for your sister,' she said. 'If they don't get you released, I will commit murder on somebody and commit suicide. I want to see Nicoline here as fast as possible. What the lawyer wants is money and carrying your baby will facilitate things.'

For some time I was silent and miserable. She wanted to hear me make a comment, but I was silent. 'Don't have fear,' she continued, 'for the law of this country gives priority to children, then to woman, followed by the men. The baby I carry now is a reason for your freedom. They will free you if you want. Know that I love you so much and I hate to see you in pains and in this desperation.'

'Did you contact Stoney before coming here?'

'No, I was frustrated. In confused ideas of compassion, I couldn't let him know but I hope to do so as soon as I get back home.'

'Well, tell him how this place looks like and also give him

the invitation letter. Tell him to process it.'

I heaved backwards to relax. Then the idea of Tina being pregnant refreshed.

'For how many months have you been carrying this baby?'

'About a month,' she said and kissed me though I was absent minded. 'Baby,' she promised, 'I will remain glued to my words. I will never let you down until the day we shall part this world. I love you.'

An officer darted from a room as if I was on a run and said, 'Your time is getting over. Madame, you should be getting out of here now.' There was a peephole from a monitoring room. When I coincidentally looked at it, I discovered that someone had been watching us and listening too. When my eyes caught up with his, the image disappeared.

'Someone has been watching us from that hole,' I said.

'I don't care,' she answered. 'That's how my people behave but I'll teach them that I'm daughter of this soil and a future mother.' She kissed me again but Woods suddenly entered and pushed my lips from hers. She was annoyed.

'Are you crazy?' she abused hitting the officer.with her hand. He dragged her into the corridor that was leading to the camp exit. I heard her in a high voice wishing the officer bad luck. 'Why do you treat people in this land like pigs,' she asked rhetorically. 'You better travel and see how others welcome strangers warmly. God will pay you in your own coins. Satan will get you baptised. You angel of darkness!' Her voice faded backwards as I walked after the security officer.

Back in the prison room, there was no one. My mates were down the cellar arranging files, door hinges and some others were carving toys from wood and other materials. Such materials would be exported and the rest for domestic use.

Those who opted to work in the cellar had several

choices of food. They had the right to cook the food given them. Every building had a kitchen that was always congested. Either one was cocking rice, or Irish potatoes. If not, it was corn powder and tomatoes source. Thus, camp life was labouring at the cellar daily from 7 pm to 4 pm, one hour to relax in a guarded place, one hour for sports, then back to the room. At the basement, there was light for the whole day.

When I entered the room, I slapped myself on the bed and burst into tears. I was chucking in joy. I fell into deep thoughts.

Let the earth rotate and let other objects face the sun. This is a dream come true. Nicoline will soon come to Europe. I will see how these cowards will send me back. Tina is a blessing in my life. God will bless her abundantly. Stoney should be happy for this good news. Things will never be the same in this life. God never created man from His own image to have permanent tribulations.

My mates could tell from my look that there was some success in the air. I never told any of them what it was. Joy could not permit me to go out that day for sports. I couldn't eat nor could I bathe. I started thinking that it wasn't a period of incarceration but one of transformation and deliverance.

Later on, an officer opened the door. 'You'll be taken to the embassy tomorrow. You must quit this country as fast as possible,' he said, banged the door, then keyed it and left. We sat discussing with Akey and others.

'You have to take courage and also meditate deeply,' said Akeh.

'My God is in control. No matter where they will take me to, the Lord is my refuge and fortress. I declare that I shall go and return tomorrow safely.'

The hours were speeding. My head fell and I was deep asleep. I dreamt terribly. The foetus in Tina's womb appeared like a big baby and spoke to me.

'Father,' it said, 'never abandon me. Never quit from my mother. Children like me nowadays face problems. Their fathers especially in this country escape after their achievements. If I grow up in this up-side-down society without you, I shall be useless. Please, I'm your blood.'

The dream continued in a more frustrating manner. 'Tell him,' said Tina to the foetus in her womb, 'because they are sometimes like mad caps but forget that blood follows the owner to wherever he goes.' Then the foetus replied to its mother, 'Yes, mama, I shall love my father and I shall follow him to enjoy a better and free life. A life of total liberty where there shall be no malignancy. Mama too shall come with me to Africa and we shall all die there. If not, we shall find life too difficult for this environment is contemptible. We shall not be needed in this society...'

I woke up. It was completely dark. I stretched my hand to the switch and pressed it on. It was 5 am. I was still in bed meditating expecting the security officer. Analysing the dream seemed frustrating. 'What is the meaning of this?' I thought. 'How can a foetus talk? That's strange. No matter what happens, I'm already a father.'

An officer soon opened the door.

'We are leaving now for your embassy. Are you ready?'

'Yes, Sir. I'm ready.'

I walked after him and he opened the gates one after the other and we were soon at the last one. There, he said to me, 'You must be handcuffed.'

'What?' I yelled. 'Don't bring havoc here, huh!' he threatened, 'or I'll do it forcefully.'

A man descended from the car and walked towards the gate. I relaxed my hands. He forced them behind and got them handcuffed. Then, an officer from outside opened the last gate. They dumped me at the back of the car and crossed me with seat belts. The car soon edged on to the traffic and we drove off. They all sat in front and each of them spoke no word to the other. Through the forest, we reached the high way and there, the car paced like never before. They all lit their cigarettes and appeared more serious. I was in trouble for I was not a smoker. I was in suffocation. 'What do you gain from these malicious acts?' I shouted. 'You better stand here and get me hanged. Don't you know no air penetrates this car?'

They looked at each other and remained mute. As we went on, the car was soon on a street that seemed to be an administrative head quarter. I saw flags on many buildings. When I saw them taking off their safety belts, I could guess the car was soon to idle. Then I saw a flag with the colours; green, red, and yellow.

'Young man,' one of them said, 'this is the embassy.' They took off the handcuffs and held me from the buckle of my belt. I walked after him climbing the stairs. At a door on the second floor was written *L'AMBASSADEUR*. One of the officers entered and informed them of our arrival for they knew we were to come. In the office was a man by name Jean Paul Pierre as he introduced himself. He took out a fax from a file.

'The German Authorities say you are Baco from Cameroon,' said Jean Paul, 'and that they want you to leave Germany. You need to confirm your name and nationality on this paper for us to prepare travel documents for you.'

'I can talk only if these people walk out of this office,' I said to the Ambassador.

'What reasons?'

'This is my country embassy and I need some freedom. Look at my hands. I have blisters all over my wrists because of handcuffs. They handcuffed before bringing me here after incarceration for no reason. Have I become a terrorist?'

'It's alright,' interrupted Jean Paul. 'Please, you should give him some freedom to talk.' They walked out. At the right corner of the table was an old man of about seventy or more. On the left was an old lady on an outdated typewriter. It was like the 1930s type.

'Are you Baco from Cameroon?' Jean Paul asked.

'Yes, Sir.'

'Do you have any documents to show that you come

from Cameroon?'

'What if I answer in the affirmative?'

'Then you have to go back home.'

'What if not?'

For some seconds, he only looked and tried to study me. I was calm at this time but he couldn't guess I was ready to burst into flames of severe aggression.

'Except you have some groundnuts for us, we are bound by law to sign that you are from Cameroon, and must go back home. Were you working here in this country?'

'Like how much money, Sir?' I pretended.

'Anything like five, six, ten... I mean anything encouraging.'

'How old are you?' I asked.

'What do you mean, young man?' he frowned.

'I mean a cockroach to kiss your smelling mouth,' I shouted. The other colleagues pressed a bell and two guards darted from a back door. Still, I stood plucky. 'Mr. Ambassador and excellent accomplices,' I warned, 'let me give you this piece of information. I have suffered in this country and I get older everyday. I have studied. I dug back home more than a pig. I've never enjoyed the natural gifts in my own country. Irrespective of the billions entering your accounts daily, you still have that audacity to ask from me money. I believe you're already an octogenarian. Yet, you linger in this office as if such is an inheritance. Time is drawing near when a tongue of the Holy Ghost fire will brush all of you. Who gave you the effrontery to ask for money?'

He asked the guards to push me out of the office but before they did, I gave him what he deserved.

'You this mammon don,' I roared, 'your lives are full of avarice. You're an Ambassador at the mammon temple and not at an embassy. I don't fear the guards. I can't go back to that crooked land.'

One other man flounced from a back door, got me buttoned and one of his hands blocked my mouth. Within a blink of the eye, I boxed, sending him to tumble on articles on the table. The old typewriter and other things fell apart. I picked up the typewriter and dashed it on the Ambassador's head. He wailed and ran into the toilet. I was ready to give him a lesson of his stupid life. Just in a few minutes, policemen appeared on the scene. Those who brought me there immediately picked and rapped me up and shoved me into the car. They joined my right leg together with my right hand so much that I coiled like a cat, before they handcuffed me. Brutally, they closed the car. Part of my dress was pinched and held by the car door. When they clipped the safety belt, I was like a chained dog with tied legs. The car galloped off like a crazy horse leading for the camp. That was another crime that would increase the volume of my file. I didn't care. I knew a heavy fine would follow.

The nearest future seemed bleak but my optimism grew more and more though zigzag. The car drove on. It was midday when we reached the camp. I never cried much from the pains. There were blisters on my hands and legs. My roommates were still down the basement working when they threw me back into the room.

I dumped my head on the bed and my eyes soon closed. Instead, I could see more than when they were open: I saw my image when I was younger playing soccer with friends. I saw myself in the days of hope with Nicoline. I saw her hips dangling and she singing a song. I saw when we used to sit on natural green fields scratching pimples on each other's face. I saw myself making her hair and singing a traditional song of love for her. I also saw her parents talking to me, advising me to take good care of their daughter. I saw mango fruits on branches, pear fruits, cocks, goats, cows, sheep and other animals in total liberty. I saw myself touching horses with smooth hairs.

Suddenly, I opened my eyes and saw a messy environment. I could feel compassion was a luxury for that environment. My heavy eyes couldn't withstand the weight of the water in it. I cried; 'Am I a man with a hundred errors? Have I done worst things than other humans do? Well, I have to submit this into the hands of God...'

I continued thinking. There was an old Bible in the room. I picked it up but never knew exactly where to read. I held it and closed my eyes.

'God forgive my sins. I've lied because of the dream for better life. I've had a deceitful relationship. I've fumbled with love. I've lied to Tina at the very time she was truthful to me. Forgive my trespasses. God, take and change my life.'

There was an interruption. The door opened. I stopped praying though my eyes remained closed. I could recognise it was the voice of Woods. I heard the door closed and footsteps surging away. When I opened my eyes, I saw four slices of sandwich bread on the table. It was only then that I recalled I never had breakfast that morning. 'Even after all I have done,' I thought, 'they still give me bread. God is in control.'

It was break time for labourers. I heard them talking and climbing up from the basement. Some were whistling. Some were singing confused hopeless songs of freedom. A majority were in pains and sorrows. Some already had their flight schedule given them. Some were waiting for their release. It was rare to hear an inmate yearning for home but Zacheous was different.

'The day I'll reach home will be one to celebrate,' he kept saying. Some were crying to reach home like him but their embassies had refused to issue documents for their return.

My mates were back from the labour room for break.

'How was it at the embassy?' Lionel asked.

'I've fought with the Ambassador and his boys.'

'Why so?' asked Akeh with hand over mouth.

'When I just saw the aged and fling stomach idiots,' I replied, 'I became so annoyed with the way they've tottered our country into a political abyss. I smashed, boxed them and was immediately dismissed.'

Okonkwo motioned his hand in appreciation of my actions and said, 'Baco, that's just what an *Oyinbu* wants. They don't like passive and calm people. As from now, they'll be most careful when talking to you. I don't give a fuck to them. I've fought for at least five times with the police. Still, there's nothing they can do to me.'

It was 5 pm that day and time for sports. The security men would play various games with inmates. Inmates too could play amongst themselves. I stood in the room meant for pool. Woods held the cue while watching inmates passing to other game rooms. It was like a sign of invitation. Okonkwo had entered the library to return a book he borrowed. He soon darted and said to me, 'fit yourself in any of the games you think is good.' He went and picked up the other cue. Woods started arranging the balls. *'I go give this stupid Oyinbu zero point today,'* said Okonkwo to me. Okonkwo was ready to strike the balls as to start the game. The whole place was noisy. Some stood watching and giving points to others in a provocative manner. After five minutes of play, Okonkwo had ten points against Woods who had two. Thus, left were only seven points. Even if Okonkwo had to leave Woods to gather all the remaining points, it wasn't going to help him. It was the second round. Lionel appeared from the table tennis room.

'I will be next if any of you is kicked out,' he said. Woods wasn't happy.

'Hey, young man,' said Woods, 'go play the table tennis you nigger.' The words rumbled Lionel's heart. 'Did I hear you say nigger?' asked Lionel. 'I'm a good man to spank you to death.'

He walked towards Woods with threatening steps. Woods dropped the cue and picked up one of the balls walking too towards Lionel. Okonkwo was muscular. He separated them from fighting but they still stood looking at each other. After a few seconds, Woods spat on Lionel. Lionel immediately picked up a ball and aimed it at Wood's face. It missed him and bounced into the next room. Then it hit on a pub dartboard breaking it into pieces. Those in the pub room rushed out to see what was happening. Woods called other security officers. They packed full the snooker room. Woods turned to Okonkwo and spat on his face after all he did to stop the fight. He was standing just a distance from Okonkwo.

'You stupid man,' said Okonkwo. 'You've spat on my face. I'm going to kill you today. You roasted pork.'

'Call me pork, or whatsoever. You're a reckless gorilla of the unknown forest.' Okonkwo also spat but it never touched Woods. 'Do you want to spit on me?' asked Woods. 'You're a useless baseless refugee, a black monkey without a home.' Okonkwo was seriously angered. He tried again to free himself but they couldn't let him go. 'You red devil, take a step to me and see what will happen to you. I had been a soldier in my country before coming here. You can't compare with me.'

Woods looked at him, sighed and said, 'It's a pity that you are a runaway soldier and a useless boy.'

The officers took Okonkwo to the cellar dungeon. Anyone who fought would spend two weeks in the cellar as punishment. 'You will be here for two weeks,' said an officer. 'What have I done?' Okonkwo asked looking at them through a small peephole. No one answered him. They keyed the door. In the small room was a spring bed with no mattress. There was also a small toilet near the bed. They would push food to him through a hole under the door like a letter into a slot. Any one sent to the cellar never had the right to watch television, go for sports or to attend camp church services. Such a person was far from minimum freedom.

While at the pub room, the Chief of the camp appeared on the scene. He saw the dartboard on the floor in pieces. He asked questions to the security men and jotted down points in a file. We wished Okonkwo be allowed to deal with Woods.

Only during sports could inmates make telephone calls.

A small telephone stand was at a corner. Only those who had telephone cards could use it. I left the scene to call Tina. When she picked the call, she was sobbing and telling me how much she loved me.

'Tina,' I said, 'you know I love you and I know you too love me. Only death can make us part. As far as I breathe in this life, you remain the lone hope that can make me feel complete. You're my excitement. Be hopeful. I doubt whether you'll come here tomorrow Saturday as we lastly discussed?'

'Yes, darling,' she responded. 'If I don't see you tomorrow, then my heart will be broken. I promise I'll be there tomorrow.'

She promised to bring for me a mobile telephone so that she could call me at will. No one, even an officer was supposed to use a mobile telephone in the camp. They were supposed to use only *walki talkis* while on duty. The only problem was how to smuggle it in. All visitors were highly controlled. The only advantage she had was that she was a woman. She promised to put it in her pant though I knew that would be impossible. She was heavy and would be difficult for the officers to discover as she thought.

Chapter Seven

Saturday was a sport and church service day. I was not to go out because Tina was to pay a visit. The early hours of every day were thinking times. Some people had thought away their brains. They were already mentally deranged. Thanks to God, I was concrete in physical condition and my brain was in order. There was only one disturbing issue; having a baby with some one I never loved even with the least fraction of my heart. Though I gave a damn to such things, there were moments I considered morals.

From 9 am to 2 pm, were visiting hours on Saturdays. Time was drawing near to the hour of 9. I woke up first and took some bread. Others were still in bed in stress of incarceration. They waited daily in agony. Many had tarried for several months so much that they never wanted to attend church services with reasons that the heavens had abandoned them. Bliss of any kind was rare to many.

As I sat on the table flipping television channels, someone opened the door. It was Woods.

'Baco,' he said in an unforgiving voice, 'someone needs you at the visiting room.'

We passed through the many gates. I saw Tina sitting on a table chair. Tina was changed. She had become more bulky. Her face was beefy than normal.

'How are you doing?' I asked looking into her eyes after she kissed me twice.

'Darling, I'm doing well. I have abundant hope as I know you are for me.'

'Have you brought the thing? No,' I asked and answered it to myself expecting her to say something.

'I've succeeded to enter with it,' she said in a low voice making sure no one heard her. At first, I couldn't believe her. She had bought the smallest size of telephone that could enter in between her laps without problems. She had forced it

71

in her ass and put on her jeans trouser. 'When I'm about to go,' she proposed, 'I'll go drop it in the toilet and you will follow to collect it. It's painful to hide in the ass, so you've to prepare your mind for that.'

'What's new around the neighbourhood?'

'You need not bother,' she said handing me a letter from Stoney. 'I went to your lawyer with Stoney and he's supposed to have appealed. He has guaranteed us. Any time from now, you'll leave this place especially as you will soon be a father. He asked for a thousand Euros and I did the transfer that same day. He also said immediately you come from here, you've to start signing documents for your stay. My grandfather also extended greetings and sympathy.'

'What of the invitation letter for my sister?' I asked opening the letter from Stoney.

'Stoney took it but I doubt whether he posted it or not.' I unfolded the letter.

'Dear Baco,' wrote Stoney, 'how is your day? I know you may say it's going badly but I want to assure you that your incarceration is just one of the negative pages you shall narrate to your children alongside your success. I pleaded for the foreign office to give me permission to visit you. Unfortunately, they turned it down. I would have taken the risk to go out of our division without permission, but since I'm in the process of the marriage deal which you best know, I fear that any crime would derail the deal. You best know what pretext they can hinge on. I do expect my passport from home to deposit for the marriage. I would have written to you before now but I had the fear that any undesirable eye could see it.

Tina and I went to your lawyer and he said things are in order. I believe that God is showering us with his abundant grace. Your lawyer asked for some money and Tina transferred to his account that same day.

I talked briefly on telephone with Nicoline. She asked me to post the invitation letter and I did it same time. The process at the embassy is going on well but they need a confirmation from Tina's grandfather. Anyhow, I feel that things shall work out.

As for Chinedu, he is fine. I don't know when, but I hope we shall meet any time from now. Take heart. I pray for you daily. In the course of praying, you too should pray for me because God attends to you more. Know that doctors are more close to patients than to those in good health. So too is God by your side. Please tear this after reading.

May God protect you. He will change your sorrows into dancing.

God bless you.'

'What has your friend said in the letter?' she asked.

'It's the same thing you've said.'

I folded it and looked at Tina. A melancholic spirit from my head went down slowly to my feet. She loved me. Perhaps, really, she did. There were moments I used to think she was a desperate and bulky dumb to think all the time that we could be couples for life. Perhaps we could be the first of couples to hold hands on streets at old age. She was in continuous admiration. She looked steadily into my eyes.

'Baby,' she said, 'you are too handsome. I love you.' I wasn't happy anyway. 'I've heard this song several times. I know you love me. I can really feel it. I see it even in my dreams. That's the reason for me accepting that you bring my sister to Germany. Why do you keep repeating this sentence all the time?'

'Darling, asking me this kind of question is like asking me why I live. My relationship with you is the only thing that empowers me. Without you in my life, I'm lost completely in this world. Just think about it. If I don't pronounce the word love daily, I feel sick. I feel stripped of a most important right. It's a word I brush my teeth with before breakfast. It gives me sight. If I don't say this word to you, I feel deprived and starved. Know that you are, and will remain the only true companion in my life.'

'That's your own way Tina. For me anything repeated many times becomes a bane. Just be calm. Remain steadfast to your oaths. You've stopped me from going home to see my love one. That alone should be enough to convey my concern. That should express my convictions.'

'Please,' she reconciled, 'don't go to extremes. The reason is that I'm drunk with love. Sometimes, I go off my mind because of too much love thought. Forgive me, if it worries you.'

There were others too discussing with their own visitors. Time was fast running.

'Time is drawing near, I think,' said Tina. 'It's better you get the phone now.'

'You can go to the toilet and I'll follow you there.'

She turned her head to see if the environment was convenient. The door that was like a gate leading to the visitors' room was often keyed. Consequently, the security officers had no fear for any free movement. Some security officers were smoking outside but watching the visitors through a glass window. Tina dashed into the toilet and I too walked there relaxed. She gave it to me and stood at the toilet door like adjusting her jeans trouser. That was just to watch if the officers' behaviour changed. Forcing the telephone in between my laps too was a stupid drama. I wore back my trouser and immediately felt some blisters. It was painful. When I walked out from the toilet, she realised my steps were not comfortable.

'Please,' I said to her, 'you should be leaving for I can't bear the pains for long.' 'I know,' she said. 'Let me go. I hope to call you immediately I reach home. I'll be back just in two days.'

She rang a bell to let them know that we had finished discussing. They came and she waved me goodbye. I was supposed to pass through a door that had an observation camera. It could dictate if one had anything like a phone with him. The officers were not too strict because only inmates used to pass there. The camera had never dictated any inmate with such illegal things. That was my target. When Woods came to lead me out of the room, my heart started pumping blood in intervals. 'After all,' I thought, 'if I am caught, there is nothing I haven't seen. My feeling for bad things done to me is already numb. They can only seize the telephone from me and throw me into the dungeon for two weeks. Only the strong ones do succeed in this kind of jungle.'

I gathered the courage and followed him towards the dark exit. One good thing that happened is that as Woods was about to open the door, his *Walki Talki* signalled. He snatched it and started talking. He even passed the surveillance room before me because he was talking joyously and laughing. As I passed fast, there was a red light for about three seconds but then, it ceased. Woods continued walking. He didn't see as he started opening the gates one after the other while still talking. We were soon at our door. When I entered the room, I felt the worst pains I ever had in life. My roommates were in a serious debate of the federal system. They were comparing non-federal states and the unjustifiable federal laws. I never had any interest. I climbed on my bunk bed and covered myself.

'What's the bad news?' Lionel asked.

'I have some cold,' I responded while adjusting and switching on the mobile telephone.

'I'm fine concerning my going back. My lawyer is doing everything to see me quit this place.'

'Baco,' Lionel advised, 'you still have to go extra might. You have to write to human right organisations to let them know that the situation back home is deplorable. These people fear to be criticised by human rights organisations or by the press. They fear their character being assassinated by the international community.'

'All these things are just a formality,' I said. 'I know it's a good idea but members of press and groups are sons of the soil, and would not bite the finger that feeds.'

As they discussed, a voice came from the loud speakers, 'Those who want to attend church services should get ready.'

Not long from then, I heard voices at the passageway. Inmates were noisily singing songs of praise and worship. Others were discussing holding Bibles waiting for any of the officers to lead them to the church hall. My roommates walked out to meet the others as they conversed. I hurriedly took out a bread knife and pierced a hole into the mattress. I made it big so much that the phone could fit into it. I stepped out immediately I forced the phone in the mattress. Woods closed all the doors and led us to the church.

There was a permanent pastor, Bruno, in the camp. He had been preaching there since 1995. There were visiting pastors too. Amongst them was Pastor Azam of the Zion Temple. He was more regular and was a powerful anointed man of God. His church was about fifty kilometres away from the prison camp. He was too devoted and he did all he could to see that through his prayers, many were released. The greatest irony was that as people were leaving the deportation prison, there was still a massive influx.

To many prisoners, Bruno was a naive man. He had the kind of protestant way of preaching. In that desperation, prisoners wanted a quaking kind of prayers, the very kind that Pentecostal men of God would crack the walls with. Azam was a Ghanaian of excellent handsomeness, height and colour. Whenever Pastor Azam was the one to preach, the church would jamb to capacity. Bruno was present in church that day but he sat to watch Pastor Azam preach.

Woods sat at a corner near those who could manage to beat the drums their own way. We all exploded in a song to warm up our voices and bodies to get ready for the word of God. We sang, telling God how we shall wear a crown when the battle shall be over. Pastor Azam joined us dancing at the altar from one corner to the other. He would change from song to song and the boys manipulating the drums would follow, though in a scattered way. Bruno stood at the back timidly shaking his body gradually. Azam motioned his hand from up downwards to gradually stop the song.

'Brothers in Christ,' he said. 'Let us put this bright and wonderful day into the hands of God. In the Mighty name of Jesus,' and we all responded, 'Amen.' He made the most powerful prayer I ever heard in my life. The prayer touched Bruno so much that he fell on the ground. Those closer to him supported him up.

'Now listen to me,' continued Pastor Azam. 'There's good news. If you believe in it, it will protect you. Good news is the same as the gospel. What I have to share with you today is that Jesus Christ died as a ransom for our sins. He died and resurrected. Because He came back to life, we are safe, halleluiah. That's the top news and that's the good news.'

There was some noise coming from behind. Many were in arguments that they would never attend services with Bruno.

'I damn the shit,' said a Nigerian. 'If they hate us, then they should never preach to us. I prefer my black brother to do it.' Pastor Azam stopped and walked to the back of the hall to ask what the problem was. Nobody spoke a word. Hasan was a Moslem. He would worship with us on Saturdays and with his Moslem brothers on Fridays. For him, he didn't care. He was frustrated and all he wanted was any means of release. After some seconds, Hasan explained to the pastor what the argument was. Azam was embarrassed. He walked to the pulpit, dropped his Bible on the lectern and said, 'Dear brothers, learn to forgive and you shall be forgiven. Love and be loved. If you believe that you are all Christians, I want to let you know, that should be the base for settling scores. Christianity is a family, a phenomenon for peace in the global world. I want to let you know that Pastor Bruno is not in any way accountable for your incarceration, nor does he know why you are here. Only the Mighty one knows why and I believe there is a good purpose for you to be here. Come on children of God. Let us sing a song for our beautiful and wonderful lives.'

An old though smooth voice exploded from the back and the drums picked it up. We were wallowing in greatest bliss. That ecstasy was rare during Bruno's preaching. He stopped the song and continued preaching.

'Don't be depressed or feel abandoned just because of the fact that you are in prison. Gold has to pass through fire before it can be bright. Joseph was sold by his own brothers as an article but he became the prime minister. Let the Lord Almighty change your situation into a big training course so that by the time you leave from here, you become Secretaries, Ministers, Prime ministers and even Presidents.' We interrupted him with roof splitting applauses. He was in top voice as if he was in the spirit and really, I thing he was.

'Children of God,' he continued, 'let me make you understand one point. If there are no torments or suffering, there shall be no testimonies. There is one thing you need to learn. You must learn how to endure in times of tribulations. Be persevering. Just get yourselves busy. Here at the prison, I've seen football and handball fields. I hear there are workshops, libraries, and rooms for other games. Keep yourselves busy and it shall be well with you. A Nigerian man, Soyinka, was held as a political prisoner several years back. While in prison, he never led his spirits down. He embarked on writing novels, one of which he titled, *The Man Died*. Several years after his release, he was recognised with the international Nobel peace prize for literature. That award carried a huge sum. Just try to imagine where he wrote the story, and you know African prisons are more catastrophic than what you find here.

There is another writer I don't know whether you know him. His name is Ngugi wa Thiong'o, from Kenya. He wrote lengthily in prison using toilet papers that were given to him. Today, he remains an indispensable force in African literature. So, my dear brothers, do not let this situation weigh you down. Use it to become something tomorrow. Every successful man has a painful story to narrate. God has not forgotten you. One after the other, you shall all leave this place, in the mighty name of Jesus.'

'... And one after the other, new people will come in,' David Willis interrupted. The whole congregation laughed. Azam too laughed shaking his head in astonishment. He continued. 'Don't think of how people shall be brought here but think that God is with humankind wherever he goes. There is temptation from Satan. There is also the test of God. Thus, in life once in a time, these things do happen but God has said *I will be with you in times of trouble.* I would like you to open your Bibles with me to *Joshua Chapter one verse nine.* It reads; remember that I have commanded you to be strong and brave. So do not be afraid. The Lord your God will be with you wherever you go... So, brothers in the name of Jesus, be strong and brave for the Lord your God will be with you wherever you go. Right here, the Lord your God is with you.'

Pastor Azam's preaching was always heart touching and life changing. That day, he made us understand that being there was for a great purpose. He quoted many people who had been prisoners but later became leaders. He also talked of John in the Bible who wrote the book of Revelations while in Prison. Having preached non-stop for about an hour, Azam was tired. There was an interlude of hot music.

'Praise God,' he said with excitement and we responded, 'Hallelujah.' 'Let me tell you something,' he continued. 'There shall always be trouble in this world. That does not mean all shall perish. Anyone who exercises his faith shall have solutions to his problems but those who think they can solve problems by making fast cash and going their own way shall never succeed. If it's not the will of God, you shall not die. Gentlemen, believe me that a plane can catch fire yet you find people coming out of it. These things can only happen if you believe that Jesus already died for our sins. This point is

79

coming up because what I've seen happening around this society is deplorable. Immigration laws have made it difficult for you and me no matter our status. It has reached a point where men go around messing up with anal sex as a means to earn a living. I know people have become millionaires. That's so embarrassing. I just hope it's not the same thing happening in this camp. Just last week, I witnessed a young boy of seventeen who was prescribed pampers by his doctor. His anus is spilling water like a fountain. Some people say a night can cost a thousand Euros if not more. Homosexuality was the cause of destruction of the city of Sodium and Gomorrah. What do you think shall happen to this city? The world is falling apart. There are thousands of venereal and airborne diseases sweeping lives. Guns are answering to bombs in Iraq, and the Middle East. Hunger and AIDS are ravishing lives in Africa. Climate has changed drastically. In Central Europe, many like you here are in incarceration. In America, anyone in a storey building is frightened at the least breeze, thinking al-Qaida might be striking again.

Some of us have deceived ladies into love and fucked them up. After marriage and establishment of a residence permit comes the disappearance act. Kids without parents wander the streets. Of almost no age, they smoke and spit and abuse the elders. They have undefined freedom given them by the laws of the country. In buses, you find them sitting and crossing their legs on the seats even when their elders stand up in the same buses without seats. It has reached a point where people make contract marriages. One pays many thousands of Euros to an old lady and she accepts him as a spouse and vice verse depending on individual cases.

I witnessed a case at the Martins hospital. A man of 34 told the federal office that he feared persecution in his home country. He changed his name, reduced his age to 16. He was successful in lying to the German Federal office. He was holder of a Bachelor Degree in Physics but this was unknown to the German government. A wealthy and lovely family adopted him according to Federal laws of adoption of immigrants below 18. This gentle man caught fever one day. The doctors' prescription was in consideration to the age of 16. He stayed in hospital for too long. When transferred to another specialist, the age was proven to be above thirty though he still argued heavily. The doctor declared that he would die within a week if the situation persisted. He made the confession that he was a man of 34 years old. That was blind cowardice. It was unfortunately late for him. He gave up the ghost on the 8th day after confession.

Dear children of God, let not the roses at bright sun deceive you. It's good to bask in the comfort of the sun from a distance. The sun is good but when one goes closer to it, it burns. My children, I am not just happy in narrating stories. I tell you all these stories in pains. See how beautiful and wonderful God has made you but some of you destroy the good work of God. You are a temple and created for a purpose. All these things happen because of avarice. If the people have decided to send you back, don't bother, be happy. Who knows whether it's the plan of God to push you to where you can succeed? You can go back to Africa and help in your own development. The continent is brain washed daily and it's a mockery on our own integrity.

I say again that our world is tearing apart. Let's think together and believe that God will protect us in the midst of these natural and manmade disasters.'

Pastor Azam became so nervous. His eyes were wet and his face solemn as if he was seeing all the troubles of the world. In that depressing mood at the altar, there was dead silence. No one could breathe. He gasped and shook his head. He sighed and starred at the sky through the window for long like a war poet at a former war front gripped in thoughts. Like a fly wiping its forelegs, he robbed his palms together hopelessly and said, 'God, forgive me. I am almost regretting why I was born to witness this deep shit of the world. God's people, do you know the sources of all ills of our society today apart from the above?'

Nobody answered. He waited for several seconds and then said, 'The simple answer is the breaking of promises. That's one of the biggest problems we face today. In the Bible, this is what we call covenants. You have the covenant of Israel, blood covenant, salt covenant, and marriage covenant. How can you tell a girl I love you and will be yours for life? After marriage and achieving what you want in this continent, you turn your backs leaving her with kids. That is a great sin. You have to pay for it severely. Countries have signed agreements to maintain world peace but have broken these agreements. Asylum laws have taken different interpretations and you find seekers in deportation prisons lingering.

My dear children, rest assured that God has not broken any of His promises. One of the most important covenants in the Holy Bible is when God says, 'I will be your God and you will be my people... See Exodus 6 verse 6 to 8. This promise of God has never, even once been breached. Who then are you to make promises and not fulfil them? I command you to stop breaking promises turning the world up side down. I command the evil spirit in you that is pushing you to mammon beliefs, greediness, avarice, and...'

His preaching that day touched and condemned me to shame. I was wondering if someone had narrated my story to him.

He stood there giving a special prayer of release. Yet, I thought of my promises to Tina and how I would break them.

'Alright,' said Azam, 'I learned that next week Friday will be a public holiday. There shall be no work at the cellar for those of you who work. I think it is good we have services that Friday because I have many prisons to visit every Saturday.'

He closed for that day and wished us well.

While in the room, I climbed up my bunk bed. David

asked me why I had to cover my head when it wasn't too cold. I told him I had some cold. It wasn't true. Under my cover, I manipulated my mobile telephone. Immediately I put it on, I received a message from Tina that had been pending.

'My passion fruit, how wonderful I feel for your existence. I wish to see you again on Friday to feel the blessing of God. Junior is doing well. Each time I touch my stomach, I feel you. I shade tears daily because of too much joy. Please reply my message. I will die for you. I love you. Kisses'

When I switched off the telephone, I wasn't in peace.

Was Pastor Azam a messenger from God? Why should he be preaching only against my plan of action? He was a religious orator only that he wanted a perfect society but no part of the present world could afford. Tina was already naming the unborn baby as junior. For me to abandon my blood was a bad thing. Nicoline too would likely come. Those were the thoughts.

There was some music emanating from the television. It was one of my favourite songs from a music channel. Tina had bought a CD with same song on it. I loved such songs with good messages. The piece of music lured me to sleep.

I heard the security officers opening doors from room to room. It was just like a dream though it was real. Woods opened our room and entered with the Chief Warder. They were like wounded lions that had felt the presence of a prey in their den. They were in great search. They searched for several minutes but saw nothing. They left but returned.

'Our telephone network is corrupted by an undesirable and unidentified electronic implement. We want the person to show up,' the Chief Warder said. Woods continued searching from one corner to the other. My heart was in serious panic. I pretended to be snoring in a deep sleep. They woke me and repeated the same question. I claimed irresponsibility. They all walked out in a mad rush search. Some other officers switched on the computers in great search. The whole camp was alert. The only thing left for me to do was to throw it out through the window but that would be only in the night.

'...the more I strive for survival and easy life, the more I gash my thoughts,' I thought.

It was dark and voices in the camp began to die down. At midnight, I took out the phone card and threw the telephone far away through the window. The rest were already asleep. Within minutes too, I was deep asleep. I dreamt heavily. In the dream, I spoke with my parents back home. At some confused moments in the dream, I saw what I had not seen for years.

'My children,' said my mother to us in the dream, 'I love you and have to tell you the truth. The only way to live a successful life is to love your parents, respect elders around you and maintain human dignity. You have to be obedient. Don't hang around off licences and bars. Don't think of gambling halls. Don't worship with mammon fans for they would initiate you. We must not ride you to big cities as other parents do. All is that we love you so much, and would love to tell you that God's time is the best. Let no one's money push you to any fascination. Never snoop at the lingering aged and disabled people for the aged are those to give you wisdom and to bless you. When you talk with your old uncles, you flavour your lives with great success...'

In the dream, when my mother stopped, my late father continued.

'...as your mother has said, there must be love amongst yourselves. If you love, some other people too will love you. Learn to be generous. There is a story I encountered when I was thirty. When I got married to your mother, I was poor. I asked for help from her parents who were better up. They gave me more than expected. From that, I gave eighty thousand francs to my small brother who was penurious. He was a good brother though broke. He took the money and invested it in a cow business. Within a year, the cow multiplied to three and it continued in that manner. By the fifth year, he had forty of those cows. That was big money. A heavy thunder and lightning blew off the little house I had. There was need for immediate reconstruction. He helped us to construct the two buildings we live in. Think of just eighty thousand francs and a reward being two houses. What a wonderful thing in my life! I tell you, select what to see, what to love, what to listen to, where to go to in this world and what to eat. Respect all, but choose your friends. Take magnanimous gestures towards your friends, but you have to be careful. Let your enemies go but see where they go because some might come back to you. Think of the good heavens first daily before you leave this house. Don't draw pictures on your bodies. Don't do piercing like the western boys. Don't promise a girl in life and later break her heart. Never sell your conscience because of money. Our old Chiefs took spirits, coats, guns… from the white men in the old days and in return gave our parents as slaves. Never tell a stranger you are so desperate. If you do, he will treat you worse than a pig if he gets your secrets…'

I woke from sleep and realised it was a dream. It was not a frightful nightmare but I was more frightened. I almost thought out my brain.

Chapter Eight

It was Friday morning and it was a public holiday. I was expecting both Tina and Pastor Azam. He had promised to hit the camp with a special prayer to see the release of many from the hopeless abyss. He had promised also to offer a special prayer for those who had their flight schedules given them. Some would fly that same week.

The sky was changing and so too the environment. Light was gradually effacing darkness and soon, one would see planes and helicopters flying high in the sky through the windows. We were on table for breakfast. Two pieces of bread, a cube of chocolate, some small quantity of jamb, and milk was available for breakfast. It was tasteless, though it was always nutritive.

'A sanctuary was changing to a centre of confusion and frustration,' said Lionel as he sighed.

'What does that mean?' I asked.

'I mean the West,' he replied. 'Coming here is coming for a Western burial.'

Willis was tired. He sighed and pounded on the door. It was time for the officers to come check if there had been any ill health during the night but none of them had come.

'Why do you slap the door?' asked Lionel.

'Why do they maltreat corpses?' Willis asked. 'Can they eat this bread?'

We laughed at his growing anger.

'We're supposed to be crying and not laughing,' groaned Willis angrily. 'What they're doing with us now is an autopsy on corpses. That is why we are obliged to visit the hospital regularly.'

There was a peephole at the door. Only someone from outside could see those inside. From inside, anyone who attempted to look through the hole would have his eyes affected by a magnifying glass. We heard the jingling sound of keys at the door. It was the Chief Warder himself.

'Who is the beast that just hit this door?' he asked. Okonkwo had not made the two weeks given him as punishment in the cellar. He was already out from there. He had been looking for a pretext to exercise his anger. He jumped from his bed and shouted at the Chief.

'Is it not a right to break this door if you don't open it on time? You all sit in your offices sipping from your coffee cups, swivelling on your chairs and refusing to open this door at the right time...'

The Chief couldn't allow him land. 'You're a mad slave condemned to death,' he said. 'I will see how you shall leave this prison.' Okonkwo looked at him with curses in his eyes and shot back, 'you roasted pork. Are you not also a prisoner?' We laughed provocatively. He was nervous and could slap. The Chief took steps backwards and said, 'I'm not supposed to exchange words with a dead prisoner. If you do this again, I'll send you back to the basement.'

'I'm a prisoner for the moment. One day I shall leave but you're a permanent prisoner as far as you continue to guard prisoners. Your joy comes from seeing people in pains...rest assured that your actions shall bear future fruits. You laugh while I cry. You shall cry when I laugh,' said Okonkwo climbing back to his bed.

We could make jokes but when Okonkwo was involved, such jokes had considerable limits. He was easily angered and when it happened, he could do the impossible things.

He suddenly jumped from his bed and dashed into the toilet, which was just a small corner in the room demarcated with some painted plywood. There were some gaps under and above for air to circulate. It was as several gunshots fired. We heard Okonkwo spreading bullets with his anus. We laughed though we were not happy. An overpowering stench of shit lurked the air. It was so strong a sent that Lionel said, 'this kind of smell can cause even a dead man's nose to move.' Willis motioned his finger in the air like a warning to Lionel because Okonkwo could behave strangely. After seconds, we heard the rubbish dripping in a greater quantity into the toilet. It was like water from a waste pipe. Then we heard him gasping in pains. I climbed to the bed and covered my head though it made no difference. Okonkwo came out appearing uncomfortable.

'I am sorry,' he said. 'I have no option but to make it. My system is not alright anymore.'

The window we had was the only source of air. It took a long time for air to penetrate. 'It's time we ask God to sacrifice a second son for the world's overwhelming troubles,' said David Willis.

Akeh asked, 'How can God do that? Has man recognised Jesus? Than regarding Jesus as Lord, nations have embarked on gun and bomb shopping and gun boot diplomacies.'

Minutes were ticking and marking the hours as it was three and some minutes after. Pastor Azam would soon be around for services. Tina had not yet come.

Woods took us to the church hall. Azam was still on the way but he had sent words. While waiting, we raised our voices praising and worshipping God. Some would dance right to where Woods sat watching. They would unnecessarily shout to provoke him. There was a boy from another block by name Clement Ash from Togo. He could preach the gospel. Indeed, he was a religious raconteur. He moved forward and said, 'Praise God,' and we responded, 'halleluiah.' 'As I introduced myself last week, I'm future Pastor Clement.'

We applauded laughing because he burlesqued like a real Pentecostal Pastor.

'I come from Togo,' he continued, 'where Presidents have learned to pass on power to their sons. The world knows there is a political problem there but people have closed their eyes and my application is unfounded. I'm on my way to Togo and I know very well they might throw me into jail when I'll reach there. I know some of you here are facing the same situation. Now, we have to tell the evil spirit that he is a liar. Let us raise our voices for God's intervention. We also have to ask for Gods protection for those whose repatriation is already a sure case... I know we come from different kinds of denominations. Make your prayers the way you want. Come on! Release, I say release...'

We started shouting in different voices in deep and powerful prayers. Some were not accustomed to praying and shouting. They dived in a worship song in low voices as others were sentencing the devil to death. Clement suddenly started praying in tongues. The Holy Spirit gripped him. He fell on the floor like one suffering from chronic fainting fit. I remained quiet just watching them. I heard a voice said *Amen*. It was Azam who was still at the passageway approaching. As he approached the last door, he dived into tongues. When he saw Clement on the floor, he laid his hand on his forehead and prayed for him.

'How many people were released during the past days?' asked Azam. 'One was released, ten sent back home and many brought in,' said a boy at the back. For about two minutes, Pastor Azam walked at the altar looking on the floor thinking of what to say. He crossed his hands behind.

'Children of God,' he continued, 'I can see you look desperate and miserable in this place. You've been complaining of eating same food daily. Some of you say even dogs are unable to eat the food given you. Some have gone insane because of continuous banging of the door.

Some have lost concentration. Someone said last week that he can no longer pray because he knows that it shall never work. He gave his reason that he was accused of drug dealing and of brutally abusing his wife after living as spouses for three years. I'm not here today to lecture on social abuses but to let you know that God is using this situation for a purpose. He is right here with you. I'm here today to say you all get set for a chronicle of testimonies.'

Nobody spoke a word. There was silence. Azam evoked melancholic spirits. The place was as quiet as a Pope's

Sanctum. 'Let me tell you one thing at this juncture. Your past does not determine your future no matter how bad your sins have been. You just need to ask God for forgiveness. He will forgive you. He will wipe your tears and restore your bliss.'

The dead silence continued. Only a few people were nodding their heads in confirmation as if such words were sinking their hearts in greater quantity. Azam walked to the back of the audience. Then, he stood at the last roll looking at David Willis who I had forced to attend the service.

'Young man,' said Azam to Willis, 'you look confused and doubting whether God would ever forgive you. Stand up.'

David stood astonished as if the pastor was saying a fact. Azam took him by the hand to the pulpit. He dropped his hand and walked with his head down for seconds. Then he raised his head and looked at the audience. 'The Lord spoke to me about this young man,' he said. 'He's looking at me to be a magician. It's no magic but the miraculous ways of the Lord. You've committed what you can call unbelievable and biggest sins. You've been thinking that going closer to God for forgiveness is a long and no success procedure. Now, all of you should listen to me.'

Azam walked to the lectern and picked up his Bible. 'Please,' he continued, 'open to the book of John chapter 5 verse 5-18,' he said licking his middle finger to facilitate the flipping of the pages.

'Any good brother should kindly stand and read it.' I rose and read, 'A man was there who had been sick for 38 years…' When I finished reading, Azam interpreted the chapter.

'Think of this man who had been sick for 38 years. He had nobody to carry him to the pool where Jesus was healing the sick. He lost hope completely. Jesus went to him and asked him, *do you want to get well?* The sick man answered, *I don't have any one here to put me in the pool… while I'm trying to get in, some one else gets there first.* Then Jesus said to him, Get up, pick your mat and walk.

Jesus never put the man in the pool before healing. He too never knew who Jesus was.'

Azam paused and suddenly exploded, 'Children of God,' he shouted. 'Shout hallelujah for the Lord is ready to surprise you as he did with the 38 year old man. Nobody will judge you before releasing you from this place. The Lord will break the gates and push you to amazing freedom.' We all shouted 'Amen,' blissfully with roof splitting applauses. 'God will shower you with uncountable testimonies and achievements. You will not follow any procedure to become a minister but you will wake up one bright morning and watch journalists on the television reading your name as a minister or president. Tell the devil that you shall not only ride in a car but in a personal plane. No matter the fact that you are in prison, God is with you. If God is for you, who else is against you? You're lions in Zion. You're conquerors…'

Azam turned to David and said, 'Young man, let the devil release you from those thoughts and set you free from incarceration. I say release, release, I say, release!' He kept motioning his hand above David's head commanding the devil to release him.

We heard a warder approaching as he talked to one of his colleagues. He went to Pastor Azam who already stopped talking as he saw the officer approaching. 'Excuse me Pastor,' he said and turned to the congregation, 'Who is David Willis?' David answered. He asked again, 'Who is Baco?' My heart pumped blood double than normal. It took me a lot of courage to answer. When David and I were walking towards him, he said, 'I have just received two faxes authorising us to immediately release these two people. So you are freed.'

The whole church exploded in joy and Pastor Azam raised his hands as he tuned a song, 'God will make a way where there seems to be no way. He walks in ways we cannot see…'

I was smiling and shivering at the same time. It was the

greatest of fumbling ecstasies. Tears sweated from my eyes but there was real joy in my heart. I was overloaded with amazement so much that I became sightless. Azam stopped the song and started bulldozing the air with prayers thanking God for His immediate answer. We were taken to the office to sign documents. 'You're obliged to report to your various foreign offices for the establishment of your temporary residence permits. Otherwise, the police could bring you here for another repatriation attempt.'

He gave us a telephone to inform our friends that we were out of prison. That was the role. I dialled Tina and told her to wait at the foreign office.

We signed all documents and stood outside the prison gate waiting for a taxi. Willis was waiting for someone he had called from the camp to pick him up. I turned and looked at the prison in a fearsome fence. It was a fence of acid rock colour like a hard rock that only a bomb could destroy. At this time, the dread rather increased. The air out of the gate was different. It was more fresh and nice.

A taxi soon idled near the gate. From there to the nearest city was about 40 kilometres. We drove off.

'Where do you come from?' asked the taxi driver as we drove on.

'From Cameroon,' I responded.

'I'm from Turkey and how long have you been here in this dirty forest prison?'

'About two weeks.' For some time, he was quiet after several questions but always looking at me in the mirror just in front and up his head.

'You say you have no residence permit and at the same time no money. What if they had refused to release you?' he asked.

'I've learned to embrace what comes my way.'

'No, that's one weakness about most Africans especially those from the west, central and south of the continent. They have self-pity and one finds them always walking on the

Western streets with pious words sharing invitations for church meetings. This is an era of agility and swiftness. Any person who wants to be a man needs to take a devil-may-care step to have money. If you see well, your continent is in financial slumber.'

'You are right,' I said, 'but you know that the times are tough everywhere. There are no more companies as used to be. Because of that, people remain unemployed.'

'I know all that lecture. Who tells you that there are no companies in this country? You don't have to think of working in a company to get rich quick. The richest people in the world are not those working in companies. Africa was a dark continent and its people continue to reason in darkness. You all have parochial and chicken hearts. You people come to this nice country and meet too much money but after about ten years, they still shove you into the planes and send you back empty handed. That's no life. Wake up, man!'

I was quiet and not understanding where he was driving to. He turned and looked at me like having something to say or expecting me to say something.

'I will introduce you to many businesses since you say you live in the same area with me.'

'I will be happy then.'

'Do you know *white*?' asked the Driver in a more serious and determined voice.

'What's that?'

'That's why I say you Africans are still in darkness. Any intelligent man can understand what I mean.'

'You can explain what you mean. Appellations vary from society to society.'

'Alright young man,' he said adjusting, 'do you know anything about narcotics, money washing or double dealing?' The entire *no* or *yes* disappeared from my lips. We were all quiet for several minutes.

'Is that what you do?' I asked looking at him.

'A hundred percent.' he confirmed.

'How do you manage it alongside taxi business?'

'Life depends on action and its modus operandi. I have boys doing it for me. If you want money to go back home, come to me and I will show you how to sell successfully.'

He handed his telephone number to me. 'See,' he said again, 'in the world, from centuries back through the dark ages until civilisation, the society is stratified. Those at the top still knit their brows to make things more right even when they are already right. What do you think of a man at the bottom? Life is short and there is a burning need to be pleasurable. This continent is good for its riches in the eye of man. Only those who can see beyond normal know that it's the darkest jungle. Many people are in a rut with both legs. They look at you to be a free rider and one who has nothing to contribute to their economy. Life can be poor, nasty and so miserable if you don't know the minds of people you meet. The more, this life you see could turn lethal if you don't know what you want. Don't wallow in painful patience when there is no hope. Don't be a mat dog that sleeps and waits for bones where no one has to slaughter an animal, or a dog that waits for bones under a vegetable stand. Do what you can do and if they don't want you here as an immigrant, you get the money and establish home with your family. I don't have a permanent stay in this country but I'm a happy man. I have three villas and four tippers making money back home. If anyone annoys me, I fuck him up and return home. So, contact me through that number within this week and I will make you rich.'

The driver said many things. He knew I was lost in the course of the discussion. He shook his head and pushed a CD in the slot. He nodded his head while repeating the sound chauffeuring further. It wasn't long when we were at the train station. He dropped me there, wished me good luck and promised to see me again.

There were many people walking up and down the stairs at the station. I saw mostly fragile octogenarians. The few young ones were together with kids of mixed races. Then at their waists, their trousers hung below their hips with part touching the ground. They were smoking and spitting at the station. Some would drink from bear bottles and splash some on the ground and at the same time abuse young girls passing by in tied jeans. I saw two policemen standing on the next rail talking in low voices and looking at me. Their eyes were cruel. They soon disappeared down the station but suddenly appeared on the same track where I had been waiting for the train. They walked passed many people coming towards me.

'Can I see your identification papers?' asked one of them.

'I'm a human being like you,' I said. 'I expect you to greet before asking me for papers.'

'It's not an obligation for me to greet you. I want to see your papers,' he insisted bringing his nose right to mine. I handed them the paper I took from the camp. They read and handed it back to me.

While at the foreign office, Tina had been happily waiting there for several minutes. She saw me from a distance, yelled fumbling and rushing to dive on me. Those on duty watched us through the window kissing. I raised my head and saw Silber. He immediately turned his head but I had caught his eyes.

'Let me see them first and we'll kiss better.'

'You better do it first,' said Tina, 'for they hate to see people in happiness.'

There were people at the waiting room. I knocked and entered. Everybody there was busy. I greeted but none of them responded. I stood for a couple of seconds. Silber turned to me from his computer and said, 'There is no one to attend to you now. If you like, you can go and come back on Monday.'

I was motionless. Mathäus walking towards another door stood near me and said, 'Stand out there. We don't need you here.'

I walked happily out of the office. It wasn't a problem for

Tina when I told her, 'They say I should come Monday.' We drove home.

The sun was already disappearing behind the high structures. The day was over but it was time young girls and boys were already making way for Night Clubs. She proposed we go to club but I turned down the idea with reasons that I had to get in touch with Stoney first.

'Why are you calm rather than happy?' She asked.

'I'm fine.'

'I'm ready to hand my life to you now and forever. If you want love, I'll give you. If you want money, I'll give you. If you want to travel round the world, I'll enable you do so. Don't be sad any longer.'

'I'm not sad. I'm just thinking of my friends here and back home that I have been missing.'

'You'll reach them if you want. There's something to gladden your heart. I had forgotten because I was overwhelmed.'

'What, you mean…' I stammered.

'Guess what. Stoney said your sister will have the visa next week. So your heart is now in peace.'

She ceased my lips with hers and I surrendered myself on the sofa. Her house telephone rang. She stretched her hand to pick it. Her lips still glued to mine.

'Answer the call first,' I grunted. She said to the caller, 'he's in the shower room. Can you call later?'

'That should be Stoney. Why have you lied to him?'

'I've been missing you so much. They can wait first,' she said dropping the phone.

'Why have you dropped the phone when it's my only friend talking?'

'I didn't drop the phone. I told him you are bathing. By the way, Stoney once told me he doesn't get too involved in your matters.'

'Since when did he say so?'

'Sometimes back when we had some misunderstandings,

97

if you can remember.' I said nothing again. We fell into actions, romancing, kissing, and doing many other activities. We would fall on the floor and then climb back to the sofa. I carried her to the bed on my shoulders, dumped her there and looked into her eyes.

'Baby,' she said in a dazzling allure like gripped by what I packed in her, 'do you know something?'

'Until you tell me my little lovely angel,' I said sucking her neck.

'I have come to the realisation that if a person believes wholeheartedly in something, it shall come to pass.'

'What do you mean?' I asked. She gasped in happiness.

'Baco, the most hopeless thing in this life is when one does not have what he deserves. The person throws himself into condemnation. He turns to curse and hate himself thinking that there is no supreme being like God.'

'What if you get what you want?'

'If you look at me now, it can answer the question. Life becomes bright like a tender tongue of fire from a birthday candle. My life is burning gradually and the smoke from it is going straight to the sky.'

'You have money. You are not supposed to complain in your life.'

'It's not only money in life that matters. Where to, with whom, and how to spend what you have is a concluding factor to define wealth. Giving too much money to somebody without people to enjoy it is just like buying ten pairs of shoes for an amputee.'

'I can understand you Tina. Let the bloom that is germinating on your cheek grow limitlessly forevermore.'

'If only that's your wish,' she said, 'because to sow a seed is one thing and to water it to bear fruits is another. I know you've given me hope and life and my grandfather will live long if he sees me in this kind of happiness. He's all I have now as a family. You know the best food for a lingering man is comfort.'

As she talked, she suddenly burst into tears. I was perplexed. I pushed her head and looked into her eyes.

'Could you be all this funny?'

'You might not understand. Life has never been fair to me,' she cried. 'I have no mother and father to pet me as parents would do. Look at me getting old at my young age. Painful thoughts have been gnawing down my muscles. I prefer to give up life than miss you. If death comes, let it take me first.'

I wiped her eyes and promised her my heart forever. I soothed her hair. She was not convinced. 'Baby,' she said, 'promise to marry me now. I hope it's not just the baby bringing us together, but also love.'

'That's what I hate to hear,' I said. 'If you like, abort the nonsense and see if I cannot remain steadfast to my words by getting married to you.'

'I don't mean to hurt you. I just want to see our relationship a living success. If you want, I can come with you on Monday and declare to them that I'm carrying your baby and that we hope to get married soon.'

'Well,' I said, 'if that can please you and your grandfather, go ahead and do it. For me, I'm comfortable.' Though she was under thought torture, she had some hopes especially the pregnancy.

I left for the camp to meet Stoney and other friends and to come back to Tina the following day. In my absence, things were the same. I rang at the door, Stoney rose from sleep.

'My tough nigger,' he shouted. 'You are a man who has defeated the lion in its den. You are a local hero. In fact, you are a Don.'

'I'm back,' I said hugging him. 'Where is tug nigger Chinedu?'

'Have a rest first before I dish for you the shocking news.'

'What could that be? I've rested more than enough at

Tina's.'

'Homosexuality is consolidating its stand and Chinedu is highly involved.'

'How can that happen? Are you sure of what you're saying?'

'Many around have knuckled down on using their anuses to enrich themselves.'

'Why has it suddenly increased this time more than before?'

'Baco, there are rumours that all those who don't have a permanent stay will have to go back either peacefully or forcefully.'

'Well,' I thought, 'maybe this idea comes from the Christian Democrats.'

'Right. The Socialists have been promising everyone a stay. Unfortunately, their voices are falling down this time.'

'A friend I met at the prison made a point which I shared with him.'

'What is the point?'

'He said some strangers are still here though without a stay because the society needs cheap labour. Now that many new members are coming in to enlarge the union, they have abundance of cheap labour even from countries that resemble them. That's why people want to use their bodies to work money so to take with them when going back.'

'Yes,' confirmed Stoney, 'he got a big point. If you're not an expert in a particular field, it will be difficult to have a visa to enter this country. They want to follow the footsteps of the States where they want only people with at least a degree to play their lottery.'

'That's the way they keep draining us but we have no option left. The leaders are already brain washed and turned up side down.'

'If God has to blink his eyes just for a second because of the bad things happening around the world, a catastrophe would be witnessed by man.'

There was a knock at the door. It was Chinedu. He was guilty. When he saw me, he shouted and exclaimed, 'Am I dreaming?'

'No,' I responded, 'your eyes are not deceiving you. I'm back to the city.'

Until midnight, we sat discussing. I narrated from one camp story to the other.

Chapter Nine

If Tina was not pregnant, and also had not promised to apply for my address to be cared to hers, or never swore that 'only death can make us part,' I would have to be in great fear that Monday morning.

It was 8 am and I sat on the sofa after a cold bath expecting Tina to bathe. It had been a busy night. She walked out of the room and said, 'Are you ready?' I nodded angrily. 'Then we can go,' she said.

'Have you bathed already?' I questioned. Her face became red as if she hated the question. Then she said, 'I am wearing my outing perfume.'

'Tina,' I shouted, 'if this relationship has to continue, you have to change from these unclean attitudes. How can you go for days without bathing after opening your legs the whole night? Are you in your senses?'

We quarrelled for a couple of minutes as she was refusing to abide. I decided to let it go. We drove off. Her perfume was a little bit irritating. Her body had an undefined odour. It was not too long when we were at the foreign office. I went in while she sat in the waiting room on a bench. I greeted them in the office. They all responded.

'What do you want?' asked Frau.

'I was asked to come here today for a visa,' I said showing her the document from prison. She whipped it like wanting to pluck off my hand, and read it keenly. Then after, they made numerous calls. For the length of two hours, they finally issued me a two weeks visa. Silber's face was like that of a wounded lion. I turned to walk out but Silber called me back and said, 'young man, this visa is no guarantee that you'll have a stay in this country. You have to look for a passport, birth certificate or anything carrying your country stamp for us to make travel documents for you. You're obliged to leave this country. Secondly, we're aware that you molested the Ambassador. If we prove you guilty of this allegation, you risk going to prison except you have to leave the country before the court issues you a summons. I'm sure you've got me well?'

I never answered him. If I did, I thought, it would be a pretext for rejecting Tina's appeal. My only answer would have been, 'to hell with your allegations, you *asshole*.'

Out of the office, Tina took the two weeks stay from me and went to the Chief. I followed her but stood at the door when she entered.

'Good morning, Sir,' she greeted.

'Good morning, young woman,' the Chief greeted back. 'What can I do for you?' Tina handed the small pass to him and said, 'That is my future husband. I wish he resides with me.' The Chief looked at the paper for long and then made several calls.

'Do you hope to get married to this boy?'

'Yes, those are my expectations. Right now, I am carrying his baby.'

The Chief was puzzled as his eyes blinked stressfully. I was already feeling bored at the door. I could eavesdrop though it was not clear what was going on.

'I want to ask you this question,' he said.

'What's it you want to ask?'

'You want to make a big mistake in your life by engaging with this boy.'

'No, Chief,' she argued. 'I'm already carrying a baby for him and I love him too.'

'Young beautiful woman, love is not only when you love a boy. I can term that as a one-sided love. Love is complete when both parties love each other. This boy doesn't love you.'

'No, he does. I'm carrying a baby for him and he must sign to have the right as the father.'

'I know what you're saying,' argued the man. 'These immigrants are freaky in attitudes. They tell you they love you just because they fear to go back home. Tell me how many times you have seen old couples of a black and a white walking on the street. That alone should mean something to you.'

'I don't care,' she continued. 'What if we'll be the first to hold hands on the streets?'

'Alright, I can understand you. Please kindly wait in the waiting room if you don't mind.' She walked out with a disappointed face and met me. I heard shoes thudding on the hard floor along the corridor. It was Frau. The Chief might have given her a call. She walked faster and slid in. I could feel sentiments of intrigues and detestation around the corner but that never bothered me much. The door soon opened again. Frau sent her head out and said, 'Tina, come for just a minute.' She walked in and the door closed.

'Tina,' said Frau, 'we all have to protect our country. You can look for a son of the soil and marry. Don't mind about the baby you carry for him. The government can declare responsibility or you declare that you'll take full care of the baby.'

'No amount of words can convince me. I remain steadfast to my oaths. How can that happen?' shouted Tina at the top of her voice.

'See,' convinced the Chief, 'the Division is ready to give you as much money as you will voice if you agree to help us send him to his country. Just allow him bring his pass and deposit for marriage and we'll use it to book for a flight for him.'

I heard Tina shouting and hitting the table. 'What a hell you are telling me to do? Do I tell you I lack money? Let me tell you this as from today. I don't know how to consume the much money I have. I don't need any further words on this issue... Now you don't want to grant my plea for his address to be changed. I'll see how you'll refuse him from becoming father of my child. I heard all of them in high voices. I couldn't persevere. I stormed the office.

'Black monkey,' thundered the Chief's voice, 'who asked

105

you to enter this office you animal of the dark forest.'

'Yes red monkey, this is my wife. I have the right to hear anything you want to tell her.'

The Chief didn't believe those words coming from me. He held me from my dress and flung me out like a valueless thing. As I stumbled out, he walked brutally after me with clenched teeth. I knew if I gave him the chance, he would lower his fist on me. I covered my eyes and slapped him three times on his face. He fell on the ground helpless. All his colleagues came out in their numbers. There were still other immigrants at the passageway waiting. Some of them walked towards the scene. The police appeared. They squeezed me and forced into the car. Tina stood there weeping.

Meanwhile, they supported the Chief to the office. Silber, Frau, Mathäus joined the Chief for a decision to be taken against me.

'…I think,' proposed Mathäus, 'we have to grant this application for change of address just to play him forget this incident. When he shall deposit any original document for paternity right or for marriage, we'll take the opportunity.'

'Or frighten him with a heavy penalty so that he can escape to another country,' said Frau.

'The Chief crossed his finger on his lips for long. He was thinking of the molestation. He coughed and said, 'all these you are saying can only work if his lawyer folds his arms. There are moments when he has a right. The best thing to do now is to contact his lawyer and propose a big sum for him. We can propose ten thousand Euros. Who hates money?'

As the Police took me away, Tina had immediately contacted my lawyer. They were unaware. However, they also contacted him almost at the same time.

Lawyer Luna was one of those who could not easily dance to the tune of money in place of Justice. If huge sums could convince him, Tina had proven her strength for the past and was still ready to do more. It was unfortunate for them. Luna's father was a British and his mother was

106

daughter of the soil. He was a gentle man of high personality and wisdom. His words were his words. One of his professional ethics was to see justice maintain its original shape and colour.

'I have as a duty to render legal services to my client according to the contract and also according to the ethics of this noble profession,' said Luna. 'I don't care whether he's a black or white. The thousand kids of mix races lingering the streets without parents is not inclusive in my duty as a legal practitioner…'

At the Police office, they kicked me from one angle to the other. They would shake me backwards and forwards. One of them headed me on my forehead and slapped me at the same time. I saw nothing but stars as I fainted. I could feel some one smashing me on my back. I was down for about five minutes. When I gained my senses, they took me into an inner room of slate colour. There, was a red light, a mattress on the floor, and a television. Close to the mattress was a toilet. That was my new home.

The following day was Tuesday. They let me go that evening. Tina was in when I rang at the door.

'Darling,' she said, 'I was really painfully missing you.' I remained silent for a while then responded, 'why can't you miss me when man keeps hunting for man?' Markuss, her dog, darted from the room like in happiest moments climbed on the sofa, and started robbing its forelegs on its snout. I was annoyed. I picked a doll and brutalised it.

'Why you do that, Baby?' grunted Tina.

'Let me tell you this for the last time. Either this dog leaves this house or I do. Why do you honour an animal than a man when Heaven has put them below?'

'No, Baco,' she pleaded, 'you're going too far. How can I honour an animal than you? Than you harm this dog, I prefer to give it back to where I bought it from.'

'Do what you want. I know I'm rivalling over a lady with a dog.'

'Darling, what are you saying?'

'Nothing, I'm not talking to you.'

Tina was uncomfortable. She knew I was unhappy and I had a reason. She could guess. 'Let's go out and enjoy some sun,' she said. 'It's bright out there.'

It was a good idea anyway. I gave Stoney a call asking whether he could join us in the city.

We soon strolled along Kama Street towards Bismarkplatz. Nearby, was river Rhein flowing to the south. Blue Ladies, where I first met Tina was there too. Part of Blue Ladies served as a day drinking spot. The apartment meant for that had a bigger space where one could sit and watch the beauty of the city. With a lift, we ascended and sat at the big veranda up the building under a canopy. Some other people sat in the open air to bask in the sun. Under the canopy, we backed the wall and began sipping from glasses of coke. From there, we saw young girls and boys in small boats on the river Rhein. There were many people with various activities on the streets. At the foot of the building, were some lame people begging food money from passers-by. In front of them were some coins in small plastic plates. They were in agony of hunger and misery. From up, I saw some men. They were three in number dressed in suits and holding Bible tracks. I saw them giving a Bible track to a man. When they passed him, he dropped it into a street trash bin. The lame people waved to them and they waved too in return.

They ascended with the lift and met us. 'Good afternoon lady and gentleman,' greeted one of them extending his hand to me. 'We're messengers from Engelische Kirche. We want to share with you about the coming of Christ. These are some tracks that can help you know more about Jesus.'

For the time they were talking to us, I spoke no word. 'If you don't mind,' one of them continued, 'we'll like to have your telephone numbers. Through that, we can invite you for our Sunday services just here in the city.'

As they discussed, I was searching for words to molest

them.

'Thanks for the offer,' I said, 'but why not give a walking stick to the lame? Haven't you seen some lame people down?' They looked at me with disappointment. 'Do you think Christianity is just an aspect of moving up and down the city with Bible tracks and your lips filled with pious words for blacks? People on the mountains should need more water than those down the valleys.'

Tina felt the humiliation. She interrupted, 'Baco, if you don't want them, tell them and stop beating around them bush.'

'Did I call them?' I shut her mouth. 'They're sons of the soil, I hope. They say the world is turning up side down. I agree. My question is, are they out pretending to turn the world up right or looking into what is causing the world to turn upside down?'

The lift near us opened and Stoney walked out of it. He saw the scene not normal. He adjusted on a seat near Tina. 'What's the matter?' he asked moving his head from face to face expecting an answer. 'I know their presence here is a pinch and blow game. Let them leave me alone,' I said. I was seriously playing to the gallery.

The scene soon caught the attention of those under other canopies. They were touching each other with their legs under the table, and then raising their eyes to those who were not aware to draw attention. My moral rectitude then was poor though I couldn't explain. I just had to behave that way to exercise my acute anger to the society.

'Gentlemen and lady,' said one of them, 'we didn't mean to hurt you. We're sorry and we have to go. Have a nice time and God continue to bless you.'

'You better leave or you have to drink this coke for me. God bless you first,' I responded. The three men took the lift and descended. Tina was angered by my reaction but I damned the shit. Stoney could understand and he was of the idea as he said, 'It's good to be of some considerable moral

109

comportment but some times too, it's good to spit on their faces as a pay back.'

I asked for a glass of coke for Stoney. He was feeling bad for what I had just passed through. He wanted to bring up same topic but I wasn't happy. 'Let's leave the topic of my arrest for home,' I said.

There were two ladies on the third table from our left with a rough haired puppy. One of them kept moving her hand on its back petting it. She would kiss it several times and sip from the flute she had in front, on the table. Stoney touched me too with his leg under the table and his head rose and fell in the direction of the two ladies. The little puppy waxed its tail and its snout touching the floor. I saw it defecating on the floor. The lady snatched out a disposable handkerchief from her handbag and picked up the faeces. It was like some pounded potatoes. She rapped it and put it in her handbag.

'What's so strange that you are all looking with a special eye?' asked Tina.

'It's a very kind lady there taking good care of a dog,' I said. 'Some other stupid ones would like to take good care of their children allowing the dogs and cats to suffer.' Tina turned her head from the scene with a sarcastic eye on Stoney.

'You don't have to curse me with your eyes. It's a good thing to care for a beautiful dog like this than a useless man like me,' added Stoney.

Tina had been admiring the puppy. She had one of her hobbies, to keep dogs. She shook her head in disappointment and asked, 'What conflict do you people have with dogs and cats?'

'Leadership conflict,' said Stoney laughing. 'Dogs will soon join other world leaders in women administration if that's what you want to know from me.' Tina smiled though with a fallen face. She sighed and supported her head with one of her hands. The topic was becoming boring. We hated dogs and cats, but she loved them madly.

'Tina,' I said jokingly, 'you should start looking for a handsome boy for my sister.'

'I hope she's not naive and timid as I used to be in those days?' asked Tina then smiling with a guilty face. 'Because of fear, I never had a boyfriend until when I met you.'

'Where was that,' asked Stoney laughing because we were at the same building.

'You're a crazy boy, Stoney. You're mad,' she said slapping Stoney tenderly.

'That day,' she continued happily, 'I can tell you people how I felt. I had been coming to this very place for several months searching for a boyfriend. That night at home, my heart was just rumbling because I was like in a fruitless dream. I was too scared.'

'Why so?' asked Stoney.

'Because I've never discussed with a black boy for all that long up to the extent of exchanging telephone numbers. I used to hear girls say they prefer the black boys to the whites. Because of that, I just developed the interest for blacks.'

'What's their reason for preferring the blacks?' asked Stoney further.

'It's so funny. They used to say the black boys are so good in bed.'

'They used to say but now what do you say?' She smiled and covered her face with her hands thrusting her tongue in between. I looked at them and smiled.

'She's more powerful in bed than I do,' I said placing my hand on her shoulders. She pushed it off saying, 'I know you're more than me. Just that you've chosen to be nutty sometimes putting me in pains.'

'Shut your mouth,' I groaned at her smiling.

The hours were rushing and we decided to leave. Out of the lift down outside, one of the lame beggars said as we were about to pass by, 'Please, I need money for bread.' His legs were weak and tiny like those of a baby though his upper torso was huge like that of a boxer. One of his hands was absent as if chopped off by leprosy.

'I have no more money with me,' I said. 'Tina, borrow me some money. I'll return it tomorrow.' Tina was astonished and then asked, 'For what do you need it?'

'Don't you see this man asking for help?'

She took out her purse and handed me some money with an angry face.

'You're not the social office to give money to people who don't work. Do you think you can satisfy everybody?'

I never cared what she said. I dropped the coins in a plastic plate in front of the lame man. Stoney used to be a crazy boy but when it came to helping such disabled, he was good. He searched his pockets and equally dropped some coins. They all said in chorus, 'God will bless you all.'

As we turned to leave, I saw a man on the opposite side of the street with a video camera focussed on the beggars. He was like a reporter. We hurried off the scene.

'The world is a funny place where people prefer to watch corpses on televisions, than spend time to help,' Stoney commented.

'Yes, that's a film for them,' I said. 'Corpses on the western streets... That's the greatest drama of the 21st century.'

Tina was too angry. She said, 'Please, I will love to leave you people. This is too much. Why do you spend time over small issues that don't even warrant the least concern?'

We were soon at the last junction and would turn right to enter Kama Street. Traffic lights changed red. We stood while cars were passing. Some children of about ten years each stood directly opposite respecting traffic. It changed green for the pedestrians to cross. The children saw us crossing. They held their noses as if they just perceived some disgusting odour. I looked at them as they waited for us to cross first. One of them flung her hand like saying, 'Go away.'

I asked them, 'Was ist hier los?' None of them answered.

Instead, I heard one of them saying to the other in their language, 'Mama says we should never go closer to them. They are monkey species and that's why they smell.'

I was cross and Stoney knew it. 'Come let's go,' said Stoney. 'I'm a good man to slap these children,' I said. I knew they had unlimited rights. Touching them would add to my problems. That's why I just let the scene fade away unregistered. We walked on. Stoney halted as Tina walked ahead.

'You know I have to go to Call Ladies today,' he said. 'In your absence, I went there and met one black lady. She comes from Nigeria and can really do that thing. She gave me twice for half the price. At least, one needs to enjoy these girls.'

'Of course, I said, 'if you stay too long without doing the thing, you likely have sperm stroke.' Stoney laughed. We took Tina home and left her there. I promised her to be back soon. I was not feeling any much hunger like Stoney for I had eaten much from Tina during the night. Tina was not happy but she had no option.

From Kama to Alt Street was about fifteen minutes. The Call Ladies building was three storeys. Under it was an internet and call shop. I entered and paid to use the net for thirty minutes. Stoney ascended and Maria was by the window smoking. At that line of rooms up the building, the prostitutes would sit besides the windows, with their breasts exposed to attract customers. Each of them had a room. She would pay this room about a hundred Euros per day whether she received customers or not. The government made it available for them. Any lady who declared that she was on sale to men would have the sales right with her prostitution license. She would use her body the way she wanted, making her own price if only she could pay the taxes.

From an opposite street, one could have a better view of how these ladies would sit with those two exposed ridges dangling on their chests, waiting for the consumers. One ejaculation was 45 Euros, while two at the same entry on the same lady could be 80. That means one could save some ten Euros. These issues were discussed freely on the streets of Germany. It had become a common practice so much so that even the prostitutes could feel free to say it in a crowd or on the streets. They were satisfied and proud of the job because it was a lucrative business.

As Stoney walked to the balcony, he saw Maria by the window. She was a tall, young, smooth, erect, and fair young woman. In fact, she was an erotic girl and physically fit for the job. She smiled and with a door remote control, she opened the door for Stoney. Before Stoney entered, she was already by her bed. Near her bed was a small cupboard with drawers. Therein were items like wine and some other stupid things like uninflected balloons. She opened one wine bottle and took out two glasses, filled and they sipped briefly. She bent down to select something for Stoney to wear on his stupid maggot thing. She stood erect to open the packet. Her hills dangled as she flung her head like a white woman to adjust her smooth hairs that were covering her eyes.

In the other rooms were ladies from other western countries. One could hear sweet erotic sounds emanating from various rooms.

'Please,' Stoney asked as she was removing a second thing for him to wear, 'what if one has to romance and kiss too? How much can that cost?'

'You've given me seventy Euros for two rounds,' she said. 'You've taken one and one is left. You have to be fast for I have customers and I need to serve them too. Come next time and we can talk about that. Know that kissing and romancing is four times more than the normal price.'

Stoney soon descended.

We left the call shop when he came. As we were walking off, Stoney was slack.

'You seem feeble,' I said. 'I'm sure you almost killed that lady with your thing.'

'Man,' he said, 'I can't deceive you. I paid for two rounds

but succeeded just one. Too much hunger instead caused me to be too weak during the game. I couldn't recover fast to pick up the second round. She had to force it with her hand and I never enjoyed it.'

Chapter Ten

Life was from one event to the other. Tina's pregnancy grew big every day. She had received letters asking her to declare the father of her baby soon to be born. Nicoline's days back home were fast ticking off. Those were the upcoming events I madly expected things to change.

To declare somebody as father of a child was one thing and for that person to be issued a stay because of the child was another.

Stoney was out of the camp. He rented an apartment while spending some days at Margeret's. I was living then permanently with Tina. The foreign office finally gave in through the efforts of my lawyer.

That Monday morning was the rendezvous day for me to fill forms that I was father of the child she was carrying. Doctor's examination was that Tina was carrying a baby boy.

It was 8 am and we took off for the office. Tina couldn't ride fast because of her condition. There were many social workers on duty. Some manipulating computers while others were busy, flipping files. When we got there, they asked us to wait outside and we sat on a bench screwed to the wall in a passageway. There were other offices in the same building.

For about an hour, we were still waiting. A lady had been ascending and descending with a lift. Each time, she would carry a pile of files as if she was transferring them. She would smile each time she passed by into a room.

'Hi,' she greeted again. 'It's been long time you are waiting here. Is there any problem?'

'There is, though not much,' Tina said. 'They say we should wait here, but they have wasted much time.'

On the lady's chest was a badge with her name *Polsizka* written on it. She walked into the office. As she walked in, Tina said, 'The name on her badge seems to be Polish.'

'Really, she looks different in shape and manner of talking. Even her nose is not too sharp like that of the

Germans.'

As we talked, I heard people whispering. I thought they were debating on something relating to us. Polsizka walked out of the office and told us, 'They say they will soon call you in. Be patient.'

As if they wanted to study something special around the place, some of them walked out of the office. I saw a huge man from an upper floor. He strolled around for some minutes and then walked into the office. My ears wagered to get what they were saying to each other. I couldn't get it well but I could guess things were not really alright. It wasn't too long when Lilian walked and stood one leg out and the other in, stretching her head to us.

'Please,' she said motioning her finger for Tina to enter. I stood up to follow Tina but Lilian stopped me while at the door. 'No,' she said, 'stay out. We'll call you in a minute.' I sat out with a coiled face. My ears were erect.

Polsizka passed back into the office. Her steps then were zigzagged.

'Your grandfather can claim to be responsible,' said Lilian, 'and you'll profit a lot from us.' I heard the voice of the huge man. He said to Tina, 'Young woman, open your heart and use your brain. I'm not talking to you just because I'm on duty. I'm talking to you like a father. Look around this society and tell me the behaviour of these strange faces. They hardly remain in a relationship after granted a stay. I've studied this boy from start to end and I know what he's out for. Don't accept this boy to be father of your child. Your thoughts shall be dashed in a deepest rut and your dreams capsized.'

I stopped breathing. 'What's the hell they're talking about?' I thought. 'I better rush in and stop them from buying her conscience else my plans will shatter.'

I couldn't immediately put that agile thought into action. I held my body tied to hear it to the end.

'We've been encouraged to have kids even if just one or

118

two,' said Tina. 'I've done my very best carrying a baby...'

'Listen, Tina,' interrupted Lilian, 'we thank you so much for your efforts. Our point is we don't want him in this country any more. If he signs as father of your kid, he does so for a stay and if he stays, he will throw you away so soon. What do you think when we shall lose our culture in two decades while other cultures shall fill the whole place?'

'Listen woman,' shouted Tina, 'if you don't like a family and a man responsible for that family, don't force others to be the same like you. I love my man and I stand by those words. I think I have to call my lawyer now!'

Tina slapped the form she was holding and rushed out to meet me in tears. I held her petting her. Lilian followed her from behind and said, 'We didn't mean to hurt you. You should all come in and sign the documents.'

'Tell me now, Miss Adviser,' she cried, 'Am I treated as a citizen of this country? Where does one find peace if not in his own country? Is this nation building or Nation destruction?'

She cried and refused signing the documents. Some ugly thoughts like wild ugly beasts rushed my mind. At that same time, I thought of Nicoline arriving just the following day.

'Don't cry Baby,' I said wiping her eyes. 'Love does not hinge on these papers we have come to sign. Love for you springs from the heart of my heart and hinges on your own heart.'

She looked directly into my eyes. We held eyes for seconds and then I said to her, 'I've said only death can alter our plans. I love you.'

'I love you too,' she said and more tears sweated from her eyes.

'Let's go back home and get ready to receive your sister-in-law tomorrow.'

We left for home. She could no longer respect the traffic. She was disillusioned. I couldn't say a word concerning the disappointment. When we reached home, there was an envelope slotted in the letterbox.

'This one is yours, Baco,' she said. I opened it and the whole page was full of figures well printed and underlined. I handed it for her to read and explain. She looked at it keenly with hand over mouth.

'What do they think they are?' she yelled.

It was a letter from the police asking me to pay the sum of eight hundred Euros for the arrest by the foreign police to the deportation camp. If I could be unable to pay, I would serve imprisonment term of one month. I was upset and I threw myself on the sofa in confusion and pain.

'Oh, strange days,' I thought. 'Shall this life ever become easy again as it was back home? Why is life too hard? Why is the world like this? Back home is synthetic and manmade spread diseases, a virus that sweeps like wildfire. Here, animals are against animals. Whites are against whites, blacks are against blacks and whites are against blacks. Even if colours become one, the world is never at peace.'

Those deep thoughts gradually lured me into a sleep. I heard Tina making several calls. It was like in a dream. I woke up and strolled to the window. I stood there watching solid structures and cars on traffic though I was not in my senses. There were buildings on the opposite street. I saw a lady too standing by her window with hands folded. From up the storey, I could watch people at a bus stop waiting for the buses. The old lady was watching down the stop.

A boy like an Arab was there at the bus stop discussing with a man who seemed to me a West African. They were like disputing over a price. The Arab boy took out several mobile telephones from his bag and handed them to the man. I watched the lady at the window. She disappeared and reappeared with a mobile telephone. She spoke strangely on her telephone and then, dropped it and continued watching the boys abnormally. Tina walked to the window too.

'What are you doing, darling?' she asked. 'I'm watching that old woman there,' I said motioning my face towards the building.

'Leave that gossip alone,' Tina said. 'She likes calling the police for people she sees doing things not understood to her. That's the work of these old people. They lack what to do and I don't understand what they gain from that.'

'I know this is a police state. Everybody is a police officer.'

I watched the boys still in arguments. Two policemen suddenly appeared on the scene. After some arguments, they handcuffed them and took them away. When they left, the old woman drew the window blind.

Thoughts were torturing me severely at the window. I had informed Nicoline that Tina was a member of a good family I met in church. She knew the kind of good boy I used to be when back home. It would be complicated for her to understand the relationship with Tina. She could swear even at the presence of a Pope that I was a good boy. Really, I used to be but life in Europe had tremendously changed me to something else.

Such thoughts robbed me of all wisdom. Indeed, the society was getting me stripped of all human egos. It was getting me emptied of all morals.

'Man knows not even $1/10^{th}$ of what he claims to know. Only God knows what future holds of man,' I thought. At this time, I was completely an opposite human being of what I had thought to become when I would reach this age. Yet, I gathered some left courage and was ready to face the storm.

The following morning, my clouded mind never left me motionless. I rose and we were prepared to receive Nicoline that early morning. At the airport, there were many people as well. We had waited for several minutes more than normal. There police were there with their normal exit control.

As I walked to relax after waiting for long, I heard, 'Baco, Baco, darling...' It was Nicoline. She fell on me with open hands like a hawk on a chick.

Tina watched us in great happiness. She could imagine the kind of family love that existed between us. There were people walking to, and fro the port. There were junkies of the land and frustrated faces too. There were also men in suits with briefcases. It was congested and as busy as a beehive. Tina hugged her as she was stretching her hand to greet.

Nicoline was more than what I had been expecting.

Every aspect of her beauty had multiplied. Her checks had developed to an expensive bloom. She was erect and well dressed in an African blouse and skirt, all of the same material. She was really cute and attractive. More than a hundred people watched us. Tina looked at Nicoline and the much beauty made her shake her head.

'Schatz, she's too gorgeous,' Tina said looking at Nicoline as if she had never seen such beauty. Nicoline smiled and asked, 'What's the meaning of *schatz?*'

'It's just a simple way of addressing a person you walk together with,' I responded in my local dialect.

We were soon at home. I took her passport. She was to return home after three months. In the course of our discussion, Tina was already telling Nicoline how she yearned for her to stay forever. She asked many questions about the people back home and the political situation. Unfortunately, Nicoline wasn't politics oriented. To her, no matter how bad a situation was, it could always be well with everybody who believed in God. For that reason, she had never in her lifetime cared to know who were those ruling the country. The only thing she knew was that, *Paul Biya is the president of Cameroon.* She had never cared to know the duties of the president of the country. The most essential thing to her was the Bible.

Tina gave me a kiss and went into the room.

'Is she pregnant, or why is her stomach like this?' Nicoline asked. Tina walked out and touched my chest. I made as if the question was not clear. Tina walked back into the kitchen. Nicoline asked again, this time with more anxiety, whether Tina was married.

'She's not married,' I answered.

'So they just like touching people all the time even people who are not their couples?' I was silent and I could feel Nicoline was somehow suspicious though she said nothing. Tina hurriedly made some fast food: bread, fried eggs and some pineapple juice.

'Please,' Nicoline said, 'I wish to have a bath.'

Tina entered the bathroom to prepare it for her. I heard her grumbling, 'Africans love to bathe more often.' She called Nicoline in and came out.

She had her bath and we took our brunch. I sat with them like a guilty criminal working on his brain on how to defend himself in a serious litigation.

'Darling,' Tina said, 'I have to rush now and transfer money for our bills. Today is the last day. If I don't do it today, I will be fined.' Then she went closer to the bathroom and said to Nicoline, 'Nico, I'll be back in a blink. I want to pay some bills.' She closed the door and left.

I was left in the sitting room alone thinking. 'If I don't tell Nicoline the whole secret now, it will soon turn to a messy situation,' I thought. I needed to do something and fast too. She was back from the bathroom. She sat looking at me and smiling.

'What's the economic situation back home?' I asked.

'It's bad but God is in control,' she said. 'People are dying back home like fowls. People are in printed and declared poverty. AIDS is ravishing almost all lives.'

'Nicoline, I love you. Do you believe me?'

'Of course,' she answered with eyes wide open, as if the question was unreasonable.

'I have something secretive to tell you now before you get perplexed. This land is the darkest jungle of the planetary system both in the known and unknown planets. Only the strong who can embrace all things on their way can survive. I've done much sacrifice for you to come to Europe. This is our life and if we manage it well, we'll make just a few years in this country and return home where we can settle…'

'Please,' she interrupted, 'tell me what the problem is all about.' I paused for a while. She was irritated.

'I hope there is nothing wrong with our relationship?' she asked.

'Until death shall make us part,' I answered. 'Nicoline, let me explain this to you. This lady is in no way as beautiful as you so much that you can say it's out of love that I am here. You can see how ugly she is but she has really fought for your coming here. Lawmakers have made the laws of this country so tight especially on immigrants. Having a child with an indigene of this country is one of the ways to have a residence permit.'

She was fast to understand that I had a relationship with Tina. She immediately started weeping. I held her hands trying to wipe tears on her cheeks.

'Baco,' she cried, 'what devil must have deceived you? Couldn't you move to another country or come back home?'

'Hey, don't shout woman. Try to understand me. These countries are in a union. My fingerprints are already here. I can't apply in another country again. If I do, they will discover me. I'm already here and I must make it here.' She was in deep tears and distress.

'Now, Baco, tell me how you shall have a mixed family. How shall your children live in a mixed milieu? Oh, God, why all these predicaments in life? Mr. Polygamy, how are you going to manage your two wives? Are you really the Baco I used to know or you're a different Baco? Can't you think of God before taking a decision?'

'I believe you will have to understand me. It's not only me doing this kind of thing. It's a general practice in the whole nation and Europe as a whole. What I expect you to do is to start thinking of how to have a stay in this country. Please, harden not your heart but try to understand me and we shall make it together. There's no turning back.'

She was still in the shock. 'How do I sit and watch my own husband cheating on me? What kind of relationship is this?'

'Nicoline, I know what you're feeling like and any human being would do the same. Many people too are married here and they have to return rings after three years or have to abandon the mother of their child after a stay is given them.'

'You wrote and called me telling me of asylum. Now the story has changed to that of marriage and the return of rings, or to that of abandoning the mother of your child.'

'I am an asylum seeker but it was never successful. That's why they incarcerated me and almost pushed me back. The authorities have implemented brutal and inhuman rules and regulations on strangers. That's why we have to go the hard way, which is the only way. It was for Tina being pregnant that they released me. You should know that I really love you and we shall die as couples. You just have to close your eyes and persevere, as we wait for the time this baby will be born. At that time, they will grant my stay and we'll be able to rent an apartment somewhere for our life. Let me not forget, she fought for your coming on condition that you're an only sister to me. She knows my engagement with her is for life. She has said her dream is to see that you have a stay in this country. If you fumble, this opportunity will fade out and our lives will be disappointing. Our success in life now hinges on this deal.'

After the long and threatening explanation, I saw the tension in her quelling down. However, it wasn't that she was convinced but for the fact that she was always peaceful. I lured her to my arms and kissed her though her whole body remained coiled. She was not fascinated by anything around her.

'Be strong, Nico,' I said. 'I had been in worse situations, but I had to familiarise myself with the baneful things of this society. That's why you still come to meet me alive.'

She heaved to her right, moving her body away from my arms.

'Why can't you understand, Nicoline? Why? Tell me.'

125

'I have heard what you're trying to explain,' she said. 'Should I stand up and dance for the cooked stories? Your behaviour this time has stripped my heart of fidelity. This has really embarrassed me. I'm telling you. I feel like killing myself.'

In about twenty minutes, she abandoned herself motionless and speechless at the same spot. She sighed and walked into the room, took out many letters and pictures and threw them on my legs. Some were from her parents and others from friends. I looked at the pictures. Little children I knew before leaving home were already big.

'Look at this your little cousin at the upper village,' I said, 'she's already big with pointed breasts.' She looked at me with annoyance. I touched her lips. 'Look at these your little beautiful lips,' I said. She smiled a little and changed back to her sad mood.

'I know I have inflicted some pain on you. It's not my aim to mar our relationship. Rather, it's a way to cement it and make things best for us.'

I kissed her again and this time, she responded by supporting my head with her right hand. I heard a key slotted in the key hole. It was Tina. My heart bombed. I jumped and sat upright on another sofa. Nicoline adjusted.

It was her habit of kissing before offering a word each time she was from outside. Sometimes, if a word would come first, it could be a simple *Hi*. Tina kissed me twice and sat on same sofa with me.

'So, Nicoline,' Tina said stretching her hand to take the house telephone, 'what are the sweet tales from Africa?' Nicoline smiled. As she conversed, Tina dialled the number of her grandfather. She talked with him for several minutes.

'Where is Stoney?' Nicoline asked.

'He lives just a short distance from here,' I said. 'I'll call him after and tell him you have arrived.

'We can visit him so I relax my legs. I'm so tired and now this trauma is coming in.' Tina could hear anything I said in

English. Thus, I talked with Nicoline in the dialect.

'As I told you it's only through the hard way that people can succeed in this country, Stoney is engaged in a secret marriage with a lady. We can't visit them except he comes here.'

'What really do you think?' she asked me in the dialect. 'How shall life look like when we shall settle?'

'You don't have to crack your brain. It shall be well. Even if I take responsibility as father of my child, the delinquent behaviour of other children will push the child away from me. Most of such children in this society do not want to accept their African parents. They call them monkeys. They are taught of the dangers of the African forest and the many illnesses from monkeys. When you must have made long here, you'll come to know that most of them are abandoned to one of the parents who is often a White.'

'I have heard all these stories you are trying to tell me back home. What I mean is how you consider humanity in relation to our culture. So you mean you have to dump the child with the mother and go your way?'

'Yes, that is the practice. I have to dance according to the music of the environment. They came to our parents, took it free and instituted bad rules, which their installed officers keep executing. They took and sold our parents like articles. They have never compensated us. Let us do what we can to grab just a pinch of the blood of our parents. Have no pity for the devil. We have to compensate ourselves.'

'What do…,' she wanted to interrupt but I stopped her.

'Listen to me. It's a thing serious and weighty. Let me tell you something I have experienced in this society. This is a society where the blind see and those who see well have dust poured into their eyes. If you want us to have jubilation at the end, close your eyes and just move your legs according to the rhythm of the sounds.'

'Well Baco, I hope you took time to grow?' she asked rhetorically. 'You never bought some years.'

'Accept greetings from my grandfather,' said Tina as she dropped the phone. 'He has said we visit him tomorrow. I know you are exhausted today.' Nicoline nodded her head. She was not aware of the death of Tina's parents. She asked Tina of her own parents and she narrated to her how they died some years back leaving her with her grandfather. As she explained, her face was fallen. Nicoline felt so sad and said to her, 'Take heart. Sometimes in life, it's not what happens that matters. What counts then is how one reacts to events because these things happen daily. It's just to believe God and take courage because He's with us everywhere we go.'

The bell at the door rang once. It was late day postman. I rushed down stairs and collected two letters. One was for me and the other, for Tina. Mine was a summons from the court. I was to appear before the court for having fought with an ambassador.

When Tina read the letter, she was not happy. 'I tell you,' she said, 'though it's good not to give a fuck to these people, you have to be careful the way you do thing things in this society.'

'What do you mean?'

'I mean the way you keep fighting everywhere you go.' She opened her own mail. It was a reminder note of the bills she just transferred in the bank.

'Is this how the country is tough?' asked Nicoline.

'I've told you,' I said in the dialect, 'you have to see it for yourself in the course of time. That's why you see people doing horrible jobs to earn a living. The country is hard especially for us. Everybody cares for himself. When I was in prison, only this lady and Stoney showed some concern. It's really a society of waist deep activities.'

'Only God can deliver his people from such a situation,' said Nicoline. 'The bad thing is that people know things that are wrong but still, they keep on. That's why man suffers much.'

'People know it and cannot cease from the practice. They

are malignant acts but at the same time, they're a source of living. I've told you, you have to look less to see more or look more to see less. You're in a society where even clergymen in some rainy days worship at mammon temples.'

As we were conversing, Tina flipped television channels. It was news time and there was a report on how a Senegalese was tortured almost to death by three white boys. They met this young man at an unholy corner and at a late hour and knifed him several times on the chest.

The same area had registered other such nasty incidents. It was for this reason that the victim set his phone on record. He was once threatened. The victim's mobile phone had recorded all what happened. On the television, they played the recorded tape.

'Nigger,' said one of the killers, 'what's up nigger? I fuck your ass nigger.'

After it played, his pictures appeared on the television. According to the reporter, the brutal boys abused him and asked him why he left his home to be a nuisance in their own country. Before the victim could blink to call the Police, they hit and knifed him several times on the chest.

The second report was a boy boxed to death by a Policeman. The boy had stolen some loafs of bread and was on the run when the shop owner called the Police. After running for one minute, the Police hit him from the back with a Police stick as he was proofing to be faster than they were. He fell on the road with the bread still in his hands.

'This is bizarre,' Tina said. 'The earlier we leave this country the better.'

'Do you want to flee your country?'

'Yes, Darling, you know what they want to do to me is tantamount to frustrating my life if not ending it.'

'That's the irony. Big countries like the States need people while this one is chasing its own immigrants.'

'No, Baco,' Tina continued, 'I don't support the United States. What they are doing is human exploitation. They have a limit to people they need in their country. Any African who wants to play the American Lottery must be skilled. If they think they are helping, why is it that they don't accept the laymen on the streets?'

'There are problems everywhere on the planet earth,' said Nicoline. 'The only way to be free is to accept Jesus as Lord. In the plane yesterday, one passenger narrated a story on how the Police shot a nurse on her birthday party in the States. Do you think the States is any better?'

As she spoke, the dimples on her cheeks pressed more in. She was looking nice. Her lips had the shape of an apple, a little bit flattened. Another thing so fascinating was her thighs. In my absence, she had developed some smooth hairs on them.

It was bedtime. In bed, I could not sleep. Tina held me but what I had in mind was Nicoline. She slept in the sitting room on a multipurpose sofa. It was surprising when Tina looked at her and said, 'Nicoline, I love the shape of your cheeks. I wish those of my Baby be just that.'

I looked at Nicoline again and I saw freshness and bloom gradually going upwards. It was like some kind of vapour.

The night was over and it was early morning. If in Africa, one could hear cocks crowing and clock birds chirping to the people, 'kweck-kwack-kwick-kwick kwe klock,' meaning, 'wake up, it is five o'clock.' Rather, it was the artificial society where the 'vuuuum' and 'wooh' sound of the fine cars and planes was the only noise. A few minutes later, the sunrays made way through the windows confirming the new day.

'Darling,' said Tina, 'I have to go to HeistLoo to buy a gift for Grandpa. We will take breakfast when I return and then leave for his place.'

'That's right Baby,' I responded because I knew she would soon leave the house. She brushed her teeth briefly and took a stick of cigarette. Tina had always hated to take a bath. However, that morning, she respected the order. She finished from the bathroom and came to dress in the bedroom. She put on just her string and kissed me before continuing.

I was thinking and watching early planes through the window high up the sky. My eyes were focused on them but my mind was somewhere else.

'How long will you be there?' I asked her.

'One hour, I think. It all depends on traffic and the availability of what I am going to buy. Driving there and back is about forty minutes.'

'I know you're feeble now but you have to be fast.' I said and she left. Then, I heard her said to Nicoline in the sitting room, 'I'll be back so soon. I want to get something for Grandpa.'

She left. I heard the car engine revived for some seconds and then she drove off. I rushed into the bathroom. Within a minute or two, I was clean and fresh. When I stepped into the sitting room to meet Nicoline, I was not myself. She was not the girl I left before going for bed. Believe me she was more beautiful that morning. I could only compare her that morning to a Swedish nymphet from a wealthy royal home. If Tina could be drunk of her beauty, one could imagine how Nicoline was. I could remember that where she was sleeping was the same chair where I first did it with Tina.

I held her tender hands on that sofa and looked at her face. I could read she had much stress. She seized her hands from me and sat up in a commanding action.

'Look, Baco,' she said, 'let me make this known to you now. Life is in stages. We loved ourselves back home. That was a stage and now, it's another. You don't have to pretend much on love words. Talk of an understanding in a foreign land and not love.'

'What do you mean?'

'If I have to start a battle with you because of this girl, it shall never end and there shall be no solution to it. It will only shatter the plans of your bought and stupid conscience.

You're a big boy. That's true but you have a small mind in the way you reason out things. If you had real love for me, you would have surrendered to return and meet me home. How can I stay to wait for you? Where is the assurance of our future, when you go around messing up with a girl who shall never be your wife? Now listen to me attentively. If you see me searching for my life somewhere else, you have to shut your mouth and try to forget of me. You just have to understand as I am doing now.'

'I know what pains and wounds you have in your heart. Even if you have a man especially a white man to pass time with, I will not bother. I understand something like a stay can come from there too. Tina is rich and if you calm down your mind, she can arrange and pay someone who can marry you and give you a stay. There are many old people close to her grandfather. Let's exploit this opportunity.' She was quiet then.

I went down on my knees and embraced her. Her eyes fell and my lips glued to hers. I felt something so nice sinking into my system and softening my heart. My eyes closed and I saw some beautiful bright stars of amoebic shape. I could not really describe how they were. Some warmth generated from my head gradually down to my bosom. I shivered several times. She too was in an allure, as her eyes remained half way closed. I moved my palm on her thighs and my muscles trembled. It was as if I was gradually sinking into water for I couldn't breathe freely. When I felt her hand searching for my buckle, I immediately assisted her. We tumbled on the sofa. In that ecstasy, she yelled in a tiny voice.

'Get up,' she said, 'your wife will soon enter.'

I rose from her and said, 'Please, say The Mother of My Child and not my wife.' She smiled as if she was happy for what she just took. I kissed her again even on her neck. When I held her ridges, some warmth too penetrated my palms.

'You know something?' I asked.

'Until you tell me...'

'You're not only beautiful. You are a piece of beauty.'

'What next?'

'So your beauty is angelic. You're smooth more than the yolk of an egg.'

'Look at your nose. Do you think you can flatter me, you this polygamous man?'

One hour and a few minutes were gone and Tina entered. After breakfast, we drove off for Grandpa. I was weak. I worked in the night with Tina and early in the morning with Nicoline but ate just little bread for breakfast. 'I should have taken something heavier,' I thought.

From a distance, we could see the antenna and the chimney pot on Grandpa's villa. Tina beeped the horn as she was at the gate. Grandpa had been waiting in the early sun on a lawn. The early summer sun was always bright.

Grandpa dangled towards the gate and opened it. He hugged each one of us. His dog waxed its tail and barked several times. He kissed and carried it with its snout touching his mouth. A family was renting the first floor while Grandpa occupied the upper part alone. We took a lift to his apartment.

Grandpa had luxurious furniture. His sitting room was of gold colour. He took us round his apartment from his sitting room to the kitchen, bedroom, bathroom, entrance room, and then to a canopy out at the balcony. There at the balcony, he would sit watching the nice cars on the street, sipping spirits.

He took us back to his sitting room. There, we saw more than an eye could see. He had three plasma modern televisions and a super hit musical set. Most of the things in the sitting room were extra grandiose. Nicoline was dumbfounded. She couldn't speak Grandpa's language and Grandpa too could not speak English. Thus, we were the intermediaries. Nicoline took out a small African bag made from synthetic fibres and handed to Grandpa. 'Greetings from Cameroon,' was the writing on the bag. Grandpa thanked her warmly. He opened it. In the bag was the sculpture of a muscular African lady.

'If it was still in the days of slave trade,' he said, 'this kind of a giant and muscular lady would be sold so expensive. But today, things have changed.'

On the central table was a small basket of small cubes of chocolate, sweets, chewing gums and others. He took out some and started chewing. Grandpa's eyes were all the time focused on Nicoline. He nodded his head in appreciation and said, 'You are cute.' Tina repeated it to her. 'Thanks for the compliment,' Nicoline appreciated timidly.

'Are you making the day here or going back with them?'

'She would have done so but for the fact that she can't communicate with you at the moment,' Tina responded.

'Is she to exhaust all the three months here or going back so soon?'

For a couple of seconds, nobody said a word. My heart shivered and my ears wagered but my heart again settled when I thought of Tina's promise to follow up with her stay.

Chapter Eleven

Time pushed us to new names. It was a month of happy birthday. Most days had become days of dispute. Things were becoming complicated. Either, it was between Tina and I, or it was Nicoline and I. Still, nature seemed to have drafted its time table as life still went on.

The baby was born and named Baco Mcbride. The newborn baby was my carbon print. As the months speeded, Tina was seriously trying to prolong Nicoline's stay as to have time to arrange a marriage deal for her.

Within six months, Tina looked for one Derik Teuer to make a contract marriage with Nicoline for the price of ten thousand Euros. Derik had accepted the amount but later on changed his mind as he developed great affection for Nicoline. He pleaded daily for me to allow him marry her for real.

He was a tall and handsome man. He promised, 'If I do not marry your sister, I will pray for God to take my life.'

I responded, 'You only need to be a strong man. She's that type of girl who can only engage with somebody who's compassionate, serious and open. Open up and Nicoline will be yours.'

Derik had been following up with a lawyer for the prolongation of Nicoline's stay. That could make him have time to sign for the engagement. Derik had become a member of the family though still to confirm. On her part, Nicoline was not happy with such an engagement. She was bitter about it. She cried all the time whenever we were just two of us. However, she never said no to Derik. She was taking it gradually though with lots of teething troubles.

One Saturday, as the sun was in a deep smile, Stoney, Nicoline, and I went to the city to relax and enjoy the bright sun. At the heart of the city was a green garden with pegged seats for people to sit and enjoy city life. There were many people there. There were kids too enjoying soccer ball, and some smoking. Nicoline was not putting on a good face.

'You look sad these days, Nicoline,' said Stoney.

'Why not,' she responded. 'Who here is happy? What kind of life are people living in this part of the world?'

'What do you mean?' I interrupted.

'Who wants to see her husband in someone's keeping? What's Baco really pushing me to do with Derik?'

'I'm not the one pushing you,' I said angrily. 'The society is pushing all of us.'

'You're not the only one, Nicoline,' supported Stoney. 'Let me advise you young woman. Never put your hands on your jaws with regrets at a war front. The people want us to be sad. Don't give up life like that. It's cowardice in life to give an enemy or rival what he wants.'

Derik had a good mastery of the city. For the short time he had made with Nicoline, he was able to locate us whenever he wanted. He had parked his car a hundred metres from the garden. I saw him approaching from a distance. He loved hugging his fiancée. He stretched his hands to Nicoline. Like a lovely but sick cat, she embraced him turning her face. Still, Derik kissed her on both jaws and then, on her lips too.

Derik chatted with us shortly and took her away and they drove off. We sat there discussing the possibilities of making a better life in Europe.

Meanwhile, Derik went home with Nicoline but was too worried. He doubted why she was too sad but could not understand.

'Can I know what's wrong with you these days?' asked Derik.

'It's my style of life. Some days make me happy while others make me sad.'

He wasn't convinced and knew something was wrong somewhere. However, he lured her on the sofa and started kissing her.

'I have a question to ask you,' she said.

'What is it? Let me hear you.'

'Why are you uncircumcised?'

'Thanks for your compliment. Is that the cause of your sadness?'

'Not a compliment but a question.'

'Is it an obligation to be circumcised?' he asked.

'Do you now answer a question by a question? Have you become an African?' she fired back.

Before they became lovers, Derik had a rough beard and so too was his moustache. His hairs were like those of a stubborn horse. Thanks to Nicoline, he shaved everything and his handsomeness was exposed. He loved to wear perfumes of stronger smells.

Nicoline coughed and said, 'Though you don't want to answer, I want to tell you this. Either we plan and circumcise that thing or we put a stop to this relationship.'

Derik was addicted to Nicoline's beauty and was ready to do anything she said. He was in a mad lust to have a child with her.

'If you accept to give me a child,' pleaded Derik, 'I am ready to do anything you ask me. My property will be willed to that child even if I'm still alive.' Derik was ready to clothe her with banknotes. He knew his wealth would keep her happy. Nicoline was always in a brainstorm of how our relation would look like.

She was a type who had attached the reading of the scriptures to her daily activities. She would get up some nights after reading the Bible, and say 'God, take me out of the mess. Rebuild my relationship. Forgive my sins and change my life.'

Chapter Twelve

My lawyer never followed the crowd. He worked waist deep for the issuance of my residence permit. He would fax to them daily explaining my right as father of the child. Thanks to him, I got a stay and a work permit.

I would only make love with Nicoline whenever Tina dashed to the shop, or to the bank. Some days too, I would rush to Derik's place when he was at work and enjoy myself with Nicoline.

It was bright outside one day and we walked towards Alt Street for the city garden. I pushed the baby trolley while Tina walked beside me. Nicoline was a few steps behind walking like a sick desert camel. As we sat on a bench in the garden, Derik called and said he would soon join us there.

Around the garden too were small bodies of created water. There were children playing with water pistols. Boys and girls sat kissing, romancing and smoking. They were fond of smoking and spitting on seats in the garden.

Stoney too had called and we asked him to meet us in the garden. When they all met us, we sat as a whole family. Stoney dashed to an ice cream kiosk and brought us ice cream.

Derik kept looking at me all the time.

'What's the matter you're looking at me all the time?' I asked. 'I admire Mcbride and just want to see the resemblance. My greatest wish is to have a child of this colour.'

'What colour?' Tina asked.

'I mean chocolate colour,' Derik responded licking the ice cream. 'The government wants to encourage childbirth but our own girls don't want it. What then do we do? We have to have these children with the blacks who share with the idea.'

'The federal government wants to deport all foreigners.

If that works, how are people who wish for such children going to do it?' I asked wanting to know Derik's mind.

'One of the main problems in this society today is that the lawmakers are blind to the changing times,' Stoney continued. 'Traditions tie down social extension. Cultures of the world are changing and any given people who refuse to change with the changing times, would have an inflexible society. That could be more dangerous. A government with tied and rigid rules and regulations would always encounter future problems.'

'That's right,' I said. 'No one can stop the earth from rotating. Anyone who tries to stop rotation can't succeed.'

As we conversed, Nicoline was not in a good mood. Neither Derik nor Tina could understand what the problem was. She kept spitting behind the bench where we sat.

'What's the matter?' Derik asked touching her on the shoulders.

'Something is irritating my system,' she replied pushing away Derik's hand. I was not happy with such attitudes. Stoney would always change a sad scene to a happy one in such occasions.

'Derik,' said Stoney stretching his hand to touch Nicoline's stomach, 'in Africa, we have the impression that when a lady sits in sun and starts spitting, she is pregnant.'

Derik smiled and said in response, 'Let that be the case.'

Nicoline was not feeling good. She spat again and started weeping. I asked her in the dialect what the problem was.

'He forces me to do stupid things in the night and now it irritates me,' she said. I shouted at her to stop and she said, 'I know the society has killed your morals but just know that any day you don't see me again, know I have returned home.'

All eyes were on me to hear and tell them what we had discussed in our dialect. I told Derik that she was not feeling fine. They insisted to call the ambulance to rush her to the hospital but I turned it down. The bright day was gradually fading and we left for home.

140

Chapter Thirteen

Every weekly day came with its own beauty and problems. A few months after I got a work permit, I had my first legal job. Selecting and classifying bottles to supply to brewery companies was never an easy task. It was a hard job. Most of us there were unskilled black labourers. It was a cold season this time. Some days were cold and wet while some were just cold with horrible temperatures going below to minus ten degrees. There was no option but to work or have your work permit withdrawn.

One of the most difficult things was how to manage the income. It was well with some months, but most months were months of crises. Wages were so unstable. Telephone, insurance, house, television, radio, and many others were some of the bills that drained all the money. According to the law, any person given paternity right was obliged to pay the sum of a hundred and fifty Euros into the account of the child from the day you are employed until when the child reached the age of eighteen. The child's account was together with that of the mother. Only the mother was able to know that the father of the child was taking financial responsibilities or not.

Tina never bordered about the small amount I had to pay monthly. That gave me an advantage to have extra money. That could enable me take a few friends out during weekends.

I would spend some weekends with Stoney and some others with other friends. It was gradually spraining the relationship. Tina had become too bitter about my habits of sleeping outside. She was putting on more weight. Even if I didn't know Nicoline, there was nothing to convince me to love such a human being. She quarrelled daily but that was making me happy. My mind for her was already dead but what to use as a pretext to leave her was still to come.

One cold Saturday morning when I returned from club, she said, 'You go around messing up with other girls. You now go out of this division without asking me because you have a stay.'

I shot back, 'You sound mad this morning. Know as from this moment that I owe no duty to sleep with you. If I do, it is out of my liking and not an obligation.'

'I'll inform your sister about this ugly attitude,' she said.

'You can inform even Chancellor Merkel of this country but before you do, get this into your blocked head. This is the last time you are nagging at me when I need my peace.'

'You asshole,' she abused. 'You refer to me as a nagging woman, not so?'

'Tina, you're the mother of my child and not my wife. Watch your lips, you ass licker. I have the right to stay in a private apartment whenever and wherever I want. Is that clear?'

'Yes, Mr. Decision maker. So this is your true colour?'

'You're right, Tina.'

'If you want to continue, I'll teach you what you've not yet learnt in this society.'

Though she always threatened, she would beg and cry for days. Making love with her was out of sympathy. She had become a desperate mother.

I decided to rent a private apartment some five hundred metres away from her but she was always ringing at my door. It was unfortunate for her because I was not in the position to rescue her from sexual starvation.

That was the beginning of another page in my history. Some weeks later, I received a letter from the foreign office informing me of irresponsibility. That same month, the doctor's report was that Nicoline was more than a month pregnant. We were in doubts whether the baby would be a black or of mixed races. Nicoline was in continuous fever. All her lips were cracked and she became ugly. Her shape at that moment was not a disturbing issue. My greatest problem was just the biological father of the baby. I prayed daily for the baby to be completely black.

I started transferring the monthly amount into Tina's account for the upkeep of Mcbride. Yet, the following month, I received another letter from the court. I became hard hearted. The court's decision that month was something an African Society would pour libations for the situation to change, but it was a common practice around a society considered a sanctuary. The judgement was lengthy but I underlined only what was really at stake.

'... Also for not caring for the child, which is the reason you have a stay,

-

-

The court declares that the child named Mcbride is under the sole care of the mother, Tina. The father (defendant) has the right to visit the child once in a month. The mother of the child must be informed a day before the day of the visit. Such information could be by telephone or by writing. The defendant must pay the sum of one hundred and fifty Euros through the mother's account monthly to take care of the child.

Failure to do all these, the state has the right to withdraw the defender's residence permit and to order for deportation to his country of origin. If not satisfied, the defendant has the right to appeal against this decision within two weeks.'

Time went on and one afternoon, I had to visit the mother of my child as we agreed on phone.

When I rang at the door, she never asked who was there. She simply opened.

'Hi,' I greeted. She did not respond but Mcbride raised his hands saying, 'Papa, Papa.'

I took him from her but her eyes were still on the television.

'Are you not sound, Tina?' I asked but she looked at me with threatening eyes and spoke no word. After several seconds, she started weeping. I was less worried. It meant nothing to me. I saw her lips shivering like she wanted to say

143

something.

'Baco,' she cried, 'where's the love you did promise me. Why have you messed me up? Why have you decided to be wicked? Please for Christ's sake, tell me.'

'I promised you a baby,' I responded smiling, 'and this is a handsome baby I have given you. How many girls in this society have a baby like this? McBride is a future minister and he is yours. You have connived with the government to take control of the child. Am I dead? I suppose you ought to be happy with the court's decision than flowing tears.'

It was more than she had thought. She looked steadily on my face like wanting to squeeze some pity. Yet, I had already hardened my heart. She was chucking with love. She was dying. But it was really unfortunate. I wasn't in the position to rescue her.

'Baco,' she pleaded, 'I'm sorry. I know I've hurt you but forgive my mistakes and come back to the house. I love you to death and you know it.'

'It's too late. You embarrassed me in court. You molested my integrity. We ought not to talk about love now but about wickedness. You don't love me, Tina. You love sex. You're a wicked girl. I believe that if I tie a penis to a log of wood, you would surely love that log. If really you loved me, you won't have gone to the extent of applying for the court to withdraw my stay and restrict me from seeing my own child daily. Tina, you are not only a wicked girl but you are wickedness in its entirety. Wickedness flows in your veins rather than blood. I'm not in any way ready to compromise this issue. So, jot it in your brain, stupid girl.'

Tina was deaf to all I said. She kept weeping and begging. She stretched her hand to hold me but I moved it off.

'Girl,' I groaned, 'take your dirty hands away you bulky beast. Why didn't you tell the court you love me? My business with you now is child business and no more. Tina, it is over. I belong to someone else and not you.'

She saw stamped seriousness in me. I could feel the words sinking into her. She knew it was a bad day. She couldn't convince me.

'Do you want to claim intelligence,' she asked. 'Let's see where you shall end. As it's too late for me, it shall also be late for you. Is this the way you want to reward me for bringing your sister and looking for her a husband? I've helped you and you know it. It's too early for you to expose your stupidity and African stereotype ideas. I'll sit you and your sister on a better seat in this country.'

'Don't just try to provoke me. You are licker of a dog's dick. Look at your stomach as that of a pregnant elephant. Let me tell you that there's nothing on the whole planet that can be fascinated with this kind of shape you have.'

'You are a monkey,' she said sobbing.

'An amoeba is better than you because it changes from one shape to the other but you are shapeless and cannot be shaped. Even none living things are scared of this kind of shape you have. You should be happy for the services I have rendered. You're a bad market. You're a heap of something still to have a name. Just take your watery ass to the dogs before I start with you now…You can take the matter to the Supreme Court or you can enter a bottle and I will cork you. Idiot.'

Tina rose to her feet and motioned her hand to the door saying, 'Leave my house or I call the police to arrest you, smelling nigger.' I kept the baby on the sofa and made for the door.

'Rather call the police to fuck your ass. You're an idiot and a nincompoop.'

She slapped the door after me almost closing my ankle.

'Never come to my house anymore,' I heard her saying. As I was descending, I heard her in a sharp voice saying, 'God why me? Why let me into this temptation. Better to take my life than let this boy abandon me.'

I was off the stupid scene. 'Did I come here to love?' I

thought. 'Could a man love an ugly animal like her? A girl whose bathe is to wear perfume.' I was in those thoughts until I reached the house. I knew summonses would follow but I didn't care.

Back home that evening, my telephone vibrated. I picked it up. It was Nicoline.

'Where are you?'

'I'm on my way to your place,' she said. 'Are you home or with your wife?'

'What nonsense are you talking about? Do I have any other wife than you?'

'I mean Tina.'

'Don't be stupid young woman. Say the mother of my child.'

Within thirty minutes, she laboured in and dumped herself on the sofa with a stressful face.

'You appear too slack, Nicoline. This is not normal.'

'It was, and is your plan to bring me and turn my life upside down in Europe.'

'Don't say so. I feel bad but this is the situation. Has Derik signed all those documents?'

'He said so but I never saw them.'

'Has the doctor made any new reports?'

'There is nothing new?'

Chapter Fourteen

Nicoline was long with pregnancy. On a Sunday afternoon, Nicoline started to labour. Derik rushed her to the hospital. At midnight that day, the baby was born. Derik called me with his mobile phone.

'Your sister is now a mother of a baby boy,' he said ecstatically.

'God is great!' I shouted. 'How is the baby doing? Is he tall like you?'

'Baco, I have a baby whether tall like me or short. Well, the midwives are in caring for the baby. I will call you again in five minutes.' He clicked off the telephone.

I turned from one corner of the bed to the other expecting a call that never came. I fell into a deep sleep and only to discover myself when it was five in the morning. Work was to start at 8 am and by 7 am, I was supposed to be on the way.

I couldn't wait. I dialled Nicoline's number but it was off. I dialled Derik's number too. It rang for several seconds but he never picked it up.

At 7 o'clock, I had not still succeeded to reach any of them. I called the office at the job side and took that day off. I asked for the hospital and took off for it.

At the reception was a lady of about forty years old. She hurriedly said and asked, 'Please, Sir, I'm the receptionist. Can I help you?'

'Yes, I wish to visit a newborn baby here by one Nicoline.' The Lady sat down and looked at me strangely. She was puzzled and I heard her stammered. 'Room 550, up the second floor,' she said.

As I climbed to the second floor, I saw a man who at first I could not recognise. It was Derik. His hairs were like the roof of a thatched house rattled by a strong wind. His head was down and he folded his arms in despair like a father whose entire family just died. He sat on a bench along the passageway, his head raised as I approached. When he saw me, his head immediately fell.

'Why in this dead mode, Derik?'

'My dreams are off the track,' he responded still with a bent head.

'What's the matter? Is the new born baby alive?' For some time he was silent. He coughed and said, 'The new born is not my child. I spent time and money nursing a woman carrying another man's baby. Can you imagine that your sister was cheating on me?'

'Derik, I can't understand you.'

'The better you don't. It's going to disrupt your imagination.'

I moved closer and held him. 'Derik, if there is something abnormal, you should tell me at once.'

'It's worse than abnormality, Baco. Nicoline has ended my peaceful life. She has delivered a black boy. She must have been going out with another man. The doctor has just confirmed it. Even naked eyes can see.'

'I don't believe you, Derik,' I said with a sad face though blissful in heart. I walked in and Nicoline was lying on the bed with eyes wide open. She had been hearing what I was asking Derik. The newborn baby was peacefully sleeping.

Derik followed from behind but never came right inside. He stood at the door. I hugged Nicoline and kissed the baby. Derik squeezed his eyes and turned off, back to the passageway. A nurse entered to take the baby for check up as was the routine. Every newborn baby had its name written on its dress, or written and attached to the wrist. That could help the nurses identify the baby and its room. Nicoline's baby had one name then.

I greeted the nurse when she entered but she never answered.

'I have to take this baby for check up. I need the baby's surname immediately,' said the nurse expecting immediate response. Nicoline looked at me. There was no answer from any of us for a couple of seconds.

'I'll name the baby later,' said Nicoline.

'You don't have a name for the baby because you don't even know the father, you prostitute,' said the nurse in her throat while walking towards the baby.'

'How does that concern you? With your wrinkled face,' Nicoline said.

The nurse wrote the name 'Nicoline' on the baby's dress. Nicoline was annoyed with the nurse's words. I calmed her down.

'You don't have to bother,' I said in the dialect. 'The true colour of the baby should soothe your mind. It should quell the heart quake that has kept you in nightmares.'

Out of a sudden, Derik swooped in. He picked Nicoline from the shoulders with clinched teeth. 'Nicoline,' he shouted, 'now tell me. You played my intelligence. What have you taken me to be? You've taken me for a gullible coward.'

I tried to untie his fingers from Nicoline but it was hard. I called for the nurses but none of them reacted. I smashed him off and he missed me three times but I gave him ugly blows.

'Nurse, Nurse, help!' shouted Nicoline. Still, nobody showed up to separate the fight. Derik took me by the legs to the ground. We held each other tied and was unable to turn.

It was not too long when the police stormed in. They took down statements from us. Derik explained that, 'I just asked why she lied to me but she and her brother joined to fight me.'

The two officers turned to Nicoline after a discussion with the nurses.

'You're still two-faced, young woman,' said one of the officers. 'This is not a society for such crooked practices. Derik and the nurses can't lie to us. Get ready for the penalty.'

They brutalised and took me to the station where I was in detention for two hours.

Derik had telephoned to Tina explaining the developments. Tina had never been in any hard terms with Nicoline. Hence, when she heard the astonishing thing, she took off for the hospital. She was flabbergasted when she met Derik in tears and the baby a black boy. From the early hours, when the baby was born, there were doubts. They didn't really know whether the child was completely black or mixed. However, in due time it was clear. The baby's ears were a hundred percent dark. The midwives too did confirm. Tina too was hopeless and desperate. She moved closer to the bed but was mute. She never greeted Nicoline but touched the baby's hand and said, 'Hello, handsome boy.' Her eyes blinked and glued to Nicoline's.

'Your brother has ended my life and you also want to end Derik's,' she said. 'Is it a plan of action?' Nicoline blinked and tears dripped. From her look, she was so blameworthy.

'Life has been unfair to me,' Nicoline said.

'What do you mean?'

'I've fallen prey to the snares of life,' she cried. 'My integrity is draining.' She looked at the baby and squeezed her eyes with her fingers. Her tears drew some feelings from Tina. She held her and soothed her hair. They were there for close to three hours. Derik could not leave. He walked in and said to Tina, 'Those are the problems of life. I thank God for Nicoline's success. She has succeeded in nailing me.'

'Tina,' she said, I must confess this to you now.'

'What do you mean?'

'The baby does not belong to Derik. Baco is the father of this baby. The secret is too big and heavy for me to carry and keep.'

Tina couldn't withstand the weight of such starkly revelations. She collapsed in front of the bed. The confession equally shocked Derik who was about to leave. Derik supported her to a chair. He informed the nurses who immediately rushed in with water and some tablets.

Nicoline narrated the story to them asking God to let her

off the trespasses. Until Tina left, she was shabby, feeble and upset.

Many hurdles set in. Life was suddenly giving way. One week later, I received two letters. One was a summons to appear before the court and the other to answer questions at the foreign office.

The court was due to sit on Friday but the foreign office had given me a rendezvous on Thursday that same week at twelve noon.

Chapter Fifteen

The foreign office was less full on Thursdays. It clocked 11.55 am. I entered the foreign office. The officers were dashing from one office to the other. Like a dog at the hole of a rat mole, Silber was waxing his tiny waist from the general room to the main office and back. It was noon at the dot and I knocked at the door.

'Yes,' said a voice that seemed to be that of Frau. I pushed it. She was alone though I had just heard several voices.

'What can I do for you?' she asked. I took out the letter sent to me and handed to her. Before she opened it, the door behind me suddenly opened. Two healthy men of giant muscles presented themselves as foreign office Police.

'Young man,' one of them said, 'you are under arrest.'

'As usual,' I responded unconsciously. They angrily bundled me to the chief of the foreign office who appeared as if he had been waiting.

'Baco,' said the chief, 'we have to take you to the court immediately and make an oral application for your incarceration and subsequent deportation. Our computer memories are full of your crimes in this society. We owe no explanation for this. The court stands a better place to do that.'

I was perplexed and those words galloped my imagination to a chucked end. I reasoned out my brain. This time, the courage in me seemed to be evaporating. They bundled me and flung into a bus.

Within three minutes, the blue bus idled near a building that was the court. They pulled me out and gripped me at the buckle of my belt. We descended through a dark passage downwards into the foundation of the building. Through a basement that was like a private car park, we ascended two floors. We were then at normal house level from where one could see other buildings through the window.

There, they pushed me into a dark room, which I can say was an unventilated waiting room of about two metres square. In there was no seat. I was there standing for two hours. When they opened the door, I saw people in an opposite room. It was the chamber of a judge, I could guess. I was taken in there. There was a man on the computer. I guess he was the registrar. There was also an old woman with green eyes. The chief of the foreign office sat near the door. I sat on the same side with Silber and Frau. They brought in a female interpreter. She was translating everything said by the judge to me.

'I am a senior judge of this court,' he said. 'This court is sitting now because of an oral application by the foreign office to deport you. The authority is accusing you of assault. You have abandoned the baby for which you are given a stay in this country.'

'No,' I cut short. 'I was issued an injunction not to step foot in the house of the mother of my child except on her consent. This, I have been doing.'

'Young man,' shouted the judge, 'this is a court and not a debate club. You've abused the very mother of your child describing her private as watery and that she carries a double stomach. Are you God? Can you create a human being? You don't feel for humanity. You can't manipulate over someone's integrity and go free. The court has decided as follows:

-Immediate incarceration at the deportation prison for a maximum period of three months awaiting deportation.

-The paternity right issued you has been automatically stripped.

- You have to pay the sum of two thousand Euros for all these services.

-You can appeal, if need be, against this decision within a period of two weeks.'

They registered the case, printed a copy of the judgement and asked me to sign.

When I got to the deportation prison, it was not strange.

It was the same place I had been. Friends I had met the first time were no longer there. The officers were the same but for a few who added. There, life was the same. Some officers could still recognise me. The chief of the deportation prison recognised the name, maybe because same name was in his computer, but doubted whether he ever saw the face.

The charismatic man of God from Zion Temple still kept visiting the camp. It was Saturday and Pastor Azam was to hold a prayer meeting with prison Christians. We were in the church hall before he came.

We closed our eyes and were in high voices asking God's interference. When Pastor Azam entered, I never realised it. I opened my eyes and the first thing I saw was Pastor Azam staring at me.

'Young man,' he said with mouth ajar. What's the problem? Are you not the one released from here sometime back?'

'I've been here, Pastor.'

The whole gathering turned their heads looking at me. I was shy. Pastor Azam walked round the hall with hands crossed behind. He spoke no word for a long time swaying his head from side to side in disappointment.

'How long are you here young man?' asked Pastor Azam.

'This is a second day.'

'What's the point behind all these?' he asked but I was quiet. After several seconds of dead silence, he said, 'Children of God, whenever you're set free from evil spirits, you have to be in continuous contacts with God. If you are not in continuous commitment with God, the devil sets again into your life. Some of you pray only when in a dark alley and when the hand of God touches and sets you free, you turn your backs on Him. Now, he is back here. Well, I don't know why you've come back here. I just want to know from you how your relationship with God has been. Have you been close to the church?'

'Sometimes,' I responded.

'And the other times what do you do? Move from one nightclub to the other?' I remained quiet. Pastor Azam prayed for all but his concern for me that Saturday was extra. He prayed powerfully so much that when I returned to the room, I continued dreaming the Holy Spirit. Like any other, the day was over.

Chapter Sixteen

My own judgement tortured me daily. I couldn't see Mcbride nor could I see the newborn, Mbah. I received a letter from Nicoline on a Tuesday afternoon and my flight was due for Wednesday.

'Dear Baco, what has happened has happened. It is of God I should say. I hope you are in good health and in contact with God. I pray for you every second and I hope God is in control. I'm out of the hospital.

Stoney handed the letter you wrote to me. I read it with understanding. You should never mind that you have to go back home. Take it as a blessing. Enclosed here is a telephone card. Please use it to call me. Mbah is wonderful in health.

My prayer is that you arrive home fast and in good health too. I think my stay here is short lived. I cannot stay without you. From the food money Derik has been giving me, I have been saving some. I already have money for the flight ticket in case I have to come immediately. While expecting your call, I wish you the best. Please be a good boy. Don't think out your brain. We have made the many mistakes and I suppose God will forgive our trespasses.'

Time was short. I couldn't give Nicoline a call nor reply her mail. The flight schedule was handed to me same Tuesday. I was to take off from the International airport, take a two hours transit in France, then to the Yaoundé Airport.

It was a safe journey that day.

Back home, I met a friend at the airport. We had schooled at same institution during our secondary school days. He rushed and gripped me with amazement. We strolled in the city for about an hour as I was seriously working on my brain.

'The way you've come shows that you're going back so soon,' said Isaac.

'Why do you say so?'

'I say so because you don't have a bag with you.'

'I may not return so soon. I have a container that must come before I leave.'

During those early hours, I could not just stoop low to Isaac but I was sure I would tell him the truth.

'Baco,' he appreciated, 'I thank God for you. If you now deal with containers, then your level has reached the apex. You are breaking even. The only favour you can give me is to connect me. I have to leave the country.'

'Don't bother. I just need a place to have a cool head. When my container shall come, we can talk about that.'

'You can be with me while waiting. What are friends for? I'm renting a two room flat uptown... How is your fiancée? We met in a small conference and Nelson told me she left the country.'

'I couldn't allow her remain here. She now has a baby.'

Isaac was happy to have met me at the airport. His greatest desire was to have connection to a visa. He took me to his house where I passed the night. I couldn't go to my home city for my pockets were a desert. Nicoline was fast in reaction. She was able to reply by e-mail and to send some money, which I could manage while at Isaac's place.

Isaac was a Christian and that Sunday was my first Sunday in the country. We left for church but I was really worried. I never knew how to start the naked truth to him. However, I followed him to church that morning. We were late. From a distance, I heard the pastor already preaching. We entered and sat.

'So, if you read Numbers chapter 5 from verse 5 on,' said Pastor Jumbe, 'you'll understand what I have been saying. Let us open to that chapter and someone should read.'

A lady sitting at the back read, 'The Lord said to Moses, 'say to the Israelites; When a man or woman wrongs another in any way, and so is unfaithful to the Lord, that person is guilty and must confess the sin he has committed. He must make full restitution for his wrong, add one fifth to it and give it all to the person he has wronged...'

When she finished reading, Pastor Jumbe cleared his voice and said, 'Dear Christians, the way out from sin is confession. If you confess with your own mouth, God will forgive your trespasses. Come on children of God, if you know anything you have done wrong confess now and ask God to forgive you.'

Although new faces gave brief introductions during the service, when it ended, Isaac introduced me more to brothers and sisters in the church. It was then I thought of giving my life to Christ. Though it was never an easy task to tell Isaac the truth, I did. He booked for an appointment with the Pastor. Jumbe informed some of his anointed ministers and they fasted and prayed for me for seven days.

Six months after, Nicoline was home. She succeeded the storm. Life at home was not easy from the start but the predicaments became historical when I had my first job with the petroleum company in Limbe, Southwest region.

It became more comfortable when I became a secretary to the managing director of same petroleum company.

Two months later, I became the President of OSYA (Organisation for the Sensitisation of Young Africans). The organisation was founded by a Cameroonian and had as one of its objectives to teach young people who still yearned to leave for the west, about the many disadvantages. It was out to encourage the youths to build their own nations and desist from the mystification of the west and other foreign countries. It had trained experts who could propose to nations how to establish companies to manage their own raw materials. It became powerful and young men from many African countries joined.